Skin and Scale

Skin and Scale

By: Camie Jo Graham

For information about permission to reproduce selections from this book, questions or comments email camie.jo.graham@gmail.com

Printed in the United States of American

ISBN: 978-0-9987738-2-7

Cover Design © 2014: Camie Graham

Cover Art © 2017: Debra Allen

Editor: Mike Valentino

© 2017 Camie Jo Graham

Skin and Scale

Chapter One

"Do I have to?" Kia asked Starlin.

"Yes, you do."

"But my mother is going to kill me.... Wait, this will never work. I've never been able to sneak up on her."

"Oh yeah, this will work. You got the paint, right?"

"Yeah, but...."

"Don't be a baby."

"But...."

"Here she comes. Are you ready?"

"No...."

"Jump!"

With the quick side step of her mother, Kia fumbled the paint and instead of the paint landing on her mother, it landed all over them.

"What are you two doing?"

"Nothing..... We're doing nothing....." Starlin said as she ran off into the woods.

"Kia..... You know you cannot sneak up on me."

"I know, Starlin talked me into..."

"Yes, my dear, I know. She is a mischievous child. I also understand she is your friend and you love her as much as your father and I." She wiped a tear from Kia's eye. "Now let us go get you cleaned up." She took a hold of her hand. "You know, next time try not to use paint."

"Yes.... *sniff*.... Mother."

The following morning Starlin walked up to my mother while we were at breakfast. She looked down towards the floor hoping she would not see her non-sympathetic smile. "Sorry about yesterday. It will not happen again." As she spoke she had slipped her hands behind her back and crossed her fingers. After the apology she ran off into the other room as she winked at me on her way out. Starlin's hair is long and black and her eyes are mossy green. Her skin is fair with freckles on her cheeks and nose.

A few months ago I was out playing in the woods around the lake nearby my home, when I heard someone crying. I searched around until I came across a little girl covered in soot with the smell of smoke all around her. The girl told me her parents and brother died in a fire while she was out picking white angel flowers for her father. She further told me that the fire had started when her village was raided by the Shades.

The Shades are what we know as a part of the Dark Master who uses its shadow as a weapon to do his bidding. Their eyes are the only thing anyone sees before they die, one eye is red and the other one is blue. Only few have survived an encounter with the Shades. No one has ever seen the master who controls the Shades.

I brought her home to meet my mother the Queen of Skins and told her Starlin's story. Later that same night I heard my mother conversing with my father the King of Scales as she convinced him to let Starlin live with us. Over the next few months, she became my sister and my best friend.

Four years later my mother got really ill, after a visit to the village Tebar, where she was stabbed in the leg by a Shade. My father did everything in his power to stop her from slipping away, but nothing he could have done would have saved her.

Six years have passed since my mother's death. I was older now and tired of sitting in a castle like a prisoner, forced to deal with the image of her all over the castle walls. I wanted to see more of the world and I thought attaining twenty years of age, I had the right to do so. My father always opposed me leaving, he did not like the idea of losing his daughter. He put two guards outside of my room and made sure that I always had escorts keeping an eye on me.

My father knows everything there is to know about me, except for one thing. I was keeping a secret from my father, I have the ability to fly. I learned how when I was really little watching Scales learning to fly outside the castle walls. While I was watching the younglings from my window I yelled to the Master Scale to come to my window so I could ask him a question. When he flew up to my window I asked if he would be willing to teach me to fly like the younglings. "I cannot teach you to fly for you do not have wings, princess. However, I can give you this amulet that when you wear it and the moon is full you will be able to fly for that night. During the full moon I can come back and teach you to fly, princess."

Several months had passed and I thought I had gotten pretty good at flying when I decided it was time to leave. I asked one of the young guards if he could get my sister for me. He only nodded and walked off in the direction of my sister's room. My stomach started to flutter, then my heart began to race. When Starlin came into my room I grabbed her hand, closed my door, sat her on my bed and explained to her what I was going to do. She stared at me wide eyed with a smile ear to ear. "Can you keep this a secret from Father?" All I could get out of her was bouncing up and down while giggling and a head nod.

That night at dinner I asked my father if he would allow me to leave the castle one last time with the promise of returning. "No! Guards, escort Kia to her room without dinner," he said furiously as he slammed his tail on the floor.

It had been more than several hours after my father

had finally gone to bed. I was contemplating how I could leave the castle without him knowing. I heard Starlin outside my room talking to the guards. I had no idea how long she had been out there talking to them, all I could hear was, "May I go in and see my sister?"

I was thinking that this was the last time I was going to see my father. Even though I never did have any intentions of returning once I had left. I was getting giddy with excitement and nervous with fear. Starlin walked into my room with a bag of belongings and helped me gather up some of my things. "Are you ready to go?" she asked happily.

As we walked towards the window I stopped and started to cry. "I can't do this. I can't leave Father."

Starlin just smiled, "Come on, baby." She grabbed my hand and pushed me out of the window as wings appeared on my back.

Chapter Two

In a small cottage three miles outside of a town called Scold Ren the sun was rising from behind the pine trees. I rolled out of bed. Groggy, I stumbled making my way to the window. After pushing the shutters open, I rubbed my eyes and noticed the fog in the air was making it hard to see past the first tree. It was as though the clouds had kissed the ground and I could smell the cold fresh dew.

I heard pounding on my front door, and a female voice frantically imploring, "Open up.... Please be home.... Please open up."

I quickly got dressed and headed towards the front door.

"Kia, you better open this door now!"

Right then I knew who it was, I felt relived it was my younger sister Starlin.

"What is she doing here so early in the morning?" I questioned myself.

"Stop talking to yourself and open this door now!" With a pound on the door I jumped.

"All right, hold on."

I unlocked the door and turned the knob as Starlin shoved the door open and threw me onto the ground. My heart was pounding as several fire arrows flew past us and hit the wall.

"What's going on, Starlin?" I demanded to know, startled as another arrow smashed into my house.

"I'll explain it all when I know we are not being attacked."

"Attacked! What are you talking about? What do you mean we? What did you do now?"

"I'll explain that later, right now we have to leave."

"Well, if we need to get out of here, we need to take the passage. It does not look like we will be leaving the easy way."

As I was speaking several more arrows whizzed through the door with one landing by my head. Staring wide eyed, I pushed Starlin off me, rolled over to the wall and stood up. We slowly made our way to my room as I closed the door and locked it. My heart pounding even more now and unsure what was going on, I closed the shutters. "Help me lift my bed to the window." Out of breath I reached for the rug covering the trapdoor.

I pulled a necklace out from around my neck, while fumbling I grabbed the small key that was attached to the chain. I leaned over and started to unlock the trapdoor, when I heard windows breaking and footsteps in the hallway. "Starlin, what is going on?" As I was speaking Starlin pushed my hand aside to finish unlocking the trapdoor. She grabbed the padlock and jumped down the hole in the floor. I quickly rolled down just in time as my bed against the window fell and I closed the door.

Even though the passageway was only three miles outside of town, it looked a lot longer. It was lightly lit by oil lamps. I asked Starlin again as we ran, "What did you do now?" Still I got no answer from her, instead she just grabbed my hand and started to run faster. I remembered why I never used the passage to get into town. I had always hated how it smelled like rotten flesh and dead rats. All was silent except for our heavy breathing and our footsteps as we ran.

Starlin and I were what felt like three fourths of the way down the passage as we heard the trapdoor break and more footsteps echoing behind us. I started to breathe even heavier, and my vision was getting blurry which made me trip over my feet. I landed face first next to a dead rat.

Starlin snatched my hand and helped me up. "No tripping now, we need to get out of here."

When we finally reached the other end I could hear the footsteps getting closer, too close. I looked behind me and I could see a faint outline of a small figure in the far distance. I grabbed my necklace and unlocked the door. As I was locking the door behind us I asked again, "Why are we running?" But I did not realize how quick the thing chasing us was as it pounded on the door right after I had gotten it locked. I jumped backwards and stumbled over Starlin.

There were not that many people out, for it was still the dead of morning. We ran into the first public place that was open. The tavern called 'Spell Cast' was still quiet inside. The odor of vomit in the air was not that pleasant. We only saw two people sitting at the bar talking to the redheaded wench running the counter. The man sitting on the left looked as though he was taller than the other. As we walked past them I choked on how bad they smelled. They looked as though they had just gotten into a fight, which reminded me of Starlin.

She is always getting into trouble even when she does not mean to. No matter how or with whom she gets into trouble with she always finds her way out. This time however I think she is in deeper than she has ever been before.

We took the farthest table away from the door and not near a window, sitting down facing each other so we both could keep an eye on the door.

"I have a few questions for you. What is going on? Why did you come to me?" I asked aggressively.

"Calm down, calm down. I'll answer your questions."

The wench walked over to our table. Her hair was

tangled and dirty with straw.

"Would you two like something?" she asked as she placed one hand on the table and her other hand on her hip.

"No thank you, we will be on our way shortly," Kia said kindly.

She walked off into the kitchen in a huff. "She seemed mad that we did not want anything," Starlin said as she watched her walk away and I noticed a white angel flower in her hair.

"Where do you supposed she got that?"

"Got what?" I turned my head to look at the wench who just walked into the kitchen. Then as I turned back around Starlin looked at me as if she saw a ghost.

She shook her head as to get rid of a memory she was caught in. "Do you remember the story your mother told us when we were little?" she said now looking serious as ever.

#######

"Kia, Starlin please come here. I would like to share a story with you before you get ready for bed."

"Coming, Mother," Starlin and I said at the same time.

We ran into the throne room laughing and excitedly sat at the base of my mother's throne as my father was just sitting next to her as well.

"Now, children, I am going to tell you a story of our planet. A long, long time ago, when our planet was very young there lived many species here, but as you know the two main species were the Skins, like me and the Scales, like your father. Now these two species were always fighting with one another, they never seemed to get along. One day a female Skin named Thora wandered into the forest of the Scales seeking a flower that could only be found in the Scales' woods. She was spotted by a Scale who was on patrol nearby. The Scale arrested Thora and she was told she was to be killed for her crime of trespassing into their woods. Now this led to a long battle between the two species. The Skins were fighting to get Thora back and the Scales were fighting so they would have the right to kill her for trespassing. After a very, very long battle and many losses on both sides Thora was not killed for her crime of trespassing. Instead she fell in love with the Prince of Scales who convinced the Scales not to kill her and to be able to marry her.

"Once they were married, Thora and her King convinced the two species to become united. They succeeded in uniting the two species and they became the first rulers of the planet. As their first order as the new rulers they passed a treaty between the two species. This treaty was said that one female and one male would be married and then govern both species. When it is time for a new heir to the throne, the king will have to choose a male to take his place and a female heir will then have to take a seat on the Queen's throne to become Queen. The male and female heir would then govern the rest of our planet just like the Scales and Skins before him and her."

"What does that mean, the king will choose a male?"

"Well you see when your father can no longer govern his people or the Skins, he will have to choose a male to take his place."

"You mean Father is going to die?"

"Yes, when your father is dying, he will choose a male to take his place as king."

Kia stood up, ran to her father and gave him a hug, crying, "I don't want Daddy to die."

"Dying is a natural part of life, Kia. We all pass on

at some time. When it is my time to go, no matter what happens, I will always be with you, sweetie."

########

"Yes, what does that have to do with anything?"

"Well your father has chosen an heir to the throne."

"What? No, that can't be, not yet." Shocked I stood up and slammed the table with my hand.

"I'm sorry he already has, we need to get you back to your father so you can take your place as the Queen."

"We will go once you explain to me what is chasing you and what trouble are you in now?" I said angrily as I slowly sat down glaring at her.

"Do you remember the rest of the story your mother told us?

"Yes. If anything were to happen to the heir of the throne before she sits on the throne anyone can take her place as queen," I said sarcastically sounding like my mother.

"Will you just cut to the chase and tell me what is wrong?"

"I have the Shades after me."

"What? The Shades? Why?"

Starlin seems very calm, as though she did not seem to be worried that she had the worst thing on our planet chasing her.

"I was seeking revenge for my family." Embarrassed, she looks down and tightly gripped her pants. "I have been tracking them for weeks now. I finally had the chance to get my revenge when I overheard them talking to a fire floating over the river outside of town. I could not understand what the fire was saying to them, but the Shades nodded and said, 'The Queen's heir will soon be dead. We will hunt her and kill her before she reaches the throne.'

"The fire spoke again and the Shades just said 'Understood.' I sneezed and they looked over at me. I ran and was luckily able to get away. They followed me to you and now here we are."

I looked up for I felt like someone was watching us. The two men at the counter were indeed staring at us. They stood up, gathered all their belongings, and then slowly walked over to us.

"You better leave out the back door if you do not wish to die today," the taller of the two whispered.

Starlin stood up. "We are not going to leave because some boy covered in blood told us to."

I noticed the swords the two men had on them, they looked very familiar to me but I could not recall where I had seen them before. The door of the tavern came flying off its hinges and hit the wench who just walked out of the kitchen with a pitcher of ale. "Get out of here now, out the back door," the shorter one hastily said as they unsheathed their swords and ran towards the Shade.

We headed through the kitchen and ran out the backdoor, which led to an alley. We turned the only way we could towards the road. As we reached the street we heard a loud wail. Starlin and I stopped, we could not move. We covered our ears and crouched down into a small ball. The sound was so piercing it sent shivers up my spine. Once the wail stopped, we stood up and continued to move out of the alley and down the road.

As we ran in front of the tavern the two males were leaving at the same time. The short male grabbed me and the other grabbed Starlin by the arm. They held onto us tight, as they turned us around and kissed us. I wanted to slap him and run, but my vision was getting blurry and I couldn't move. With the last strength I had I looked over at Starlin. I saw she was passed out and the taller male was holding her in his arms.

Chapter Three

The smell of smoke was making me sick to my stomach, and as I slowly opened my eyes, I did not recognize where I was. I could feel a cold draft and I heard the sound of water dripping with loud thunder that made the ground shake. My vision was blurry and I was slightly dizzy. The ground was cold and felt very smooth. "Where is Starlin? Starlin, where are you?" I said, panicking as I felt around me.

"Stop talking so loud, I'm over here."

I stumbled over to the faint figure. She was tied up at her ankles and at her wrists. "Why are you tied up and I am not?"

"I don't know, just get these damn ropes off me." I cut her hands free with a rock I found near her, when someone walked into the cave. The person had a hood on and was standing towards the fire which was making it hard to tell who it was.

"You know you two are stronger than you think. That kiss should have knocked you both out for weeks, and here it is only six hours later." It was a male by the sound of his voice.

"Oh, I see they are awake," another male who walked into the cave, said.

As soon as I cut the ropes off Starlin's feet she pushed me out of the way, jumped over the fire and landed right on top of the male who came into the cave first. As I watched them grapple on the ground, Starlin was struggling to remain in control. It reminded me of when I was young and I would walk into the great hall of the castle and watch Starlin wrestling with a guard on the castle floor.

"Stop! I know who you two are. You are guards from the castle. I knew I had seen those swords from somewhere. Those swords are only given to the guards of the royal family."

"Now that you have figured that out, we can be on our way," the taller male said.

"No, I am not going anywhere with guards from my castle. What are your names?"

The male Starlin was grappling with threw her off him with ease as if he was letting her win the match.

"Ouch, that was rude," she said as she rubbed her butt.

He had short brown hair, green eyes with a scar across his nose and a scar on his left hand. "My name is Grend."

The shorter one sat down. I got to see his eyes in the firelight. They were red with a tint of blue, he had short blond hair and a very fair complexion for a male.

"My name is Esom. Now may we get going?"

"I'm not leaving, especially not in this storm," Starlin said as she punched Grend in the arm, while standing up. She walked over to the fire, sat down and stared deeply as if caught in a memory.

"Now you know our names," Grend said happily.

"Would you like to tell us where we are at?" I asked.

"No," Esom said.

"What do you mean no?" I was getting mad now.

"You can go see for yourself," he said as he pointed towards the back of the cave.

I stood up, turned around and saw nothing but a cave wall. I was not sure what he was talking about. I walked a few feet and raised my hand up to the wall. "There is nothing here."

Esom stood up and walked over to me. "Look." He

took my hand and placed it where I had already been touching the wall. "If you look for an exit you will not see one. You must look hard to see the entrance that is beyond the wall."

He moved my hand across the wall in a pattern. I started to feel the wall move as though it was not there to begin with. As my hand moved, I started to feel the rock becoming smoother. Which was odd for it still looked jagged and rough. The shadows from the rock slowly moved away from my hand then I saw my hand disappear. I was shocked and did not know what was going on. "Once you see the entrance it all makes sense." He walked into the wall and vanished still holding my hand as he pulled me through.

Chapter Four

"Kia, where the hell did you go?" Starlin ran over to the wall as it turned back into solid rock again. "Kia, damn you! You have to leave me here with this thing?" she said annoyed as she turned around. "I am not a thing you know."

"Shut up. Thing."

Starlin picked up a rock and threw it at Grend.

The cave wall was spinning, as it slowed down I saw what looked like stars all around me. The walls were shimmering; blue, red, yellow, green, and purple. I could not believe what I was seeing. I looked around for a way back so I could get Starlin but the cave wall was gone and in its place was a flowing waterfall.

"I have heard of this place before, I didn't think it was real. My mother would tell me stories of the cave that leads to the fairies of Ethorn."

"Do you want to see more?"

"Yes, please," I said, my curiosity piqued.

Esom started to walk forward and the walls began to move again. This time instead of spinning it was changing shape into trees. As the trees got taller I started to see light shimmering through the canopy above. The dust in the air swirled around the trees, I saw dew on the mushrooms growing at the base. We walked further into the woods and the cave disappeared, all I could see was the waterfall. I heard light laughter and singing in the distance.

I saw something pass a tree out of the corner of my eye. I jumped, turned and the image was gone. As we walked past the tall grass I put my hand out. It felt soft almost like silk. The smell of dew on the tress enhanced my senses. I was able to see, hear, and feel more than I ever had before. It was as though I was in a dream. We walked even further, this time I saw a clearing ahead of us. The canopy was gone and the sun was piercing the clouds above. Through the light rain, I saw ribbons of color streaking through the air as I watched fairies flitting from one side of the clearing to the other.

"Is this really real?"

"Yes, I have something I need you to see." He took my hand and we walked towards the center of the clearing. As we reached the center the clouds started to disappear above. The sun was getting brighter and Esom's grip was getting tighter.

"Ouch, why are you holding my hand so hard?"

"Because I don't want to lose you again."

I was shocked that he had said that. Again? What did he mean? I had never seen him before. I didn't even recall him in the castle.

As we stood in the center I started to see fairies gathering around the edge of the clearing. Esom turned me around, grabbed me by the waist and held on to me. I blushed and started to feel warm. I wanted to push him away but something was telling me not to. I closed my eyes and laid my head on his chest. He held me even tighter and looked up into the sky. The fairies who were around the border started to circle around us.

Esom pulled me away from his chest and lifted my head as if he was going to kiss me on the forehead. When I looked into his eyes I saw this time they were solid red and the blue in his eyes had faded.

When I finally noticed where we were I gasped. We were in the air and the fairies had gone back down to the border of the clearing. I could not believe what I was seeing. Esom had wings, they were huge.

"How do you have wings?"

"I was born with them."

"How did I not see them before?"

"I am able to make them change size so they are not detected by anyone unless I want them to."

I felt at ease when he told me that, it made me realize that he was a Halfling like me. Not that many Skins and Scales outside of royalty would produce offspring for it was far too dangerous to the Skin and sometimes the Scale as well.

"Your mother must have been a Scale?"

"Yes, her name was Sthora."

"What about your father?"

He stopped flying, slowly taking hold of one shoulder at a time. Making sure I did not fall, he spun me around so I was facing the other direction. What I saw took my breath away. The sun was midday and I was able to see all of my father's kingdom. I could not see the castle, however. As a matter of fact, I could not see any buildings. He spun me back around and started to dive towards the ground as I closed my eyes. He opened his wings to slow down. Fairies were flying into the clearing towards the center as if trying to catch us from hitting the ground.

When we touched the ground his wings were gone and the fairies were back at the border. He gently laid me on the grass as he kissed me ever so lightly on the lips. My vision was starting to get blurry again, I passed out in his arms.

When I woke up it was dark, and I lay in a fully red silk covered bed with white angel flowers. I saw candles lit all over the room, and the fireplace was lit and warm. The room seemed big for being in the fairy realm. The door slowly opened, I saw a female walk in.

"Kia, how could you leave me like that?"

"What are you talking about?"

"In the cave. You left and I was stuck with the dumbass who would not stop staring at me."

"I…didn't... sorry. Where are we?"

"Still in the fairy realm."

"How did you get here?"

"Esom told us what happened. He said you hit your head and passed out."

"I did? I don't recall hitting my head at all." I touched my head, there was a bump. It hurt when I touched it. I remembered flying and realizing that Esom was like me. The sun was bright and the valley was beautiful. I still could not for the life of me remember hitting my head. I looked out the window and saw a fairy sitting on the windowsill. She shook her head and flew off.

"How long have I been out?"

"A week."

"What! A week? We have to get moving."

I went to put my feet out over the edge of the bed when the room started to spin. "What is going on? Why is everything spinning?" I fell back and my head hit the bed. "Where is Esom? I have a bone to pick with him."

Starlin left the room. I was really confused about what happened. I thought it was great, but how exactly it turned from what I saw so beautiful to something so wrong was baffling. I saw the fairy again sitting in the window, this time she slowly flew into the room and came closer to me. She was sitting on the edge of the bed now and it sounded like she was trying to talk to me but I could not understand what she was saying.

I listened for what seemed like forever. I could tell at some points she was mad, then at some points she looked like she was crying then she seemed like she was happy. I was so confused by what was going on that I started to cry, thinking that I was going insane. How could I not

19

remember hitting my head?

"Stop, I cannot understand what you are saying. I'm sorry," I said as I wiped tears from my face.

"She is telling you how you hit your head and that she is mad at you for making the decision you did so many years ago. But most of all she is happy to see you and says you have grown into a beautiful woman."

I was confused. I looked at him like he was insane. How could he understand what she was saying, no one knows the language of fairies.

"How can you understand them?"

"Not for you to know. Now rest so we can be on our way to your father."

With that sentence, I started to cry again; that's right, my father is dying. I rolled over so the fairy could not see me cry. Why was I afraid of letting her see me cry?

Esom walked over to the bed. "Are you all right?"

The fairy was now touching my shoulder. She was so tiny I wouldn't have known she was there if it wasn't for the wind from her wings brushing my hair.

"Yes, I am fine." I sat up quickly. I went to slap Esom in the face, but before I could he grabbed my wrist and pushed me back onto the bed. He got really close to my face again. His eyes were changing colors, this time to a solid blue. The fairy rushed in between Esom and me. She started to speak again, and this time she sounded frantic. I was not sure what was going on, and more confused than ever.

Chapter Five

He let go of my wrist then grabbed the fairy. He was breathing heavy, his clenched hand looked as though it was getting tighter. The fairy was struggling in his hand trying to break free of his grip. She started to cry when she bit his index finger which made him drop her.

"What is going on?" Esom quickly got back on the bed, leaning over me, and breathing heavy. "You mean nothing to me," he said angrily with a growl in his voice.

He got off the bed, picked up the fairy and started to talk to her. I could not understand him, he was speaking the fairy language. I sat there completely confused and lost, he looked over at me and his eyes had turned back to the red and blue color they were in the cave. "Would you mind telling me what the hell is going on?"

"No. Now is not the time. You still need to rest from hitting your head."

I rubbed my head again and it was still sore. "I need to get to my father, we cannot sit around waiting for my head to get better. I still do not even remember hitting my head." I stood up and started to get dizzy. I was not able to keep my balance and I fell into Esom's arms.

"You really need to rest."

"Will you please tell me how I hit my head?"

"You let go of me and started to fall. That's all there was."

"I do not remember letting go of you," I said, confused as my head started to ache.

"When I turned you back around so we could go back to the ground, you told me you could fly as well and let go of me. I was trying to catch you as you fell. The fairies were trying to catch you as well. We barely caught you in time when you hit your head."

"I don't remember that. I remember we were flying back towards the ground when the fairies were flying into the clearing to help catch us for some reason or another."

"No, they were trying to help catch you."

"I really do not remember that at all."

"You told me you could fly. You said you didn't have wings as I did, but you had a secret and could fly just like me. When you let go you fell," he said aggressively.

"I really don't remember that. I do have a necklace that allows me to fly but that is only at night and when the moon is full. How did I end up here though?"

"After you hit your head, I kissed you slightly on the lips just long enough you would not be in pain anymore. Also, so you would not be asleep for a long time."

"Oh." I blushed slightly still confused on how I didn't remember that at all.

Starlin and Grend walked into the room. She came over to me and handed me water and some bread.

"Kia, you need to eat, and drink water. Grend told me that the effects of the kiss can sometimes cause memory loss."

"So, that's why I can't remember anything?"

"Yes, the effects are only temporary but sometimes it can be permanent. The effects should only last a few days," Grend said disappointed, as he looked over at Esom in great concern.

"So how long do we have to stay here? I need to go see my father."

"Two more days and you should be well enough for us to head out again," Grend said.

"I can't wait that long." Standing up I started to sway as I got dizzy again.

"You have to. When you can walk without getting dizzy we can go."

"Kia, now please get some sleep. I'll stay here with you. Grend. Esom, do you mind leaving us now?"

"Not at all." Esom bowed "If you need anything we will be right outside your door."

They turned around, walked out and closed the door. Starlin walked over to the bed and sat beside me.

"You know, we could pretend this is a sleepover?"

"But it's not. My dad's dying and I have to be there before he goes." Her eyes start to water.

"I know, Kia. We will, just give it two days for you to get feeling better. We will be there before your dad passes."

Starlin laid down next to me, put her arm over my body and we both fell asleep.

Chapter Six

As I woke up, I rubbed my eyes and noticed that I was back in the castle. I was in my room, in my bed. It was as though nothing had changed since I'd left so many years ago. "How did I get here?" I got up and walked over to the window. The sun was rising and a red and blue colored bird flew into my room and landed by the mirror. I walked over to the bird and went to pick it up. When I did, the bird flew to my door. I walked closer to it and it pulled opened the door and flew down the hallway.

Everything looked just like it did when I was young, only slightly different. "How can this be?" There was dust and cobwebs everywhere. I saw pictures of my parents and of me. The candles were melted away and some were still lit. The dead leaves that had been blown in from the open window in the hall sent a chill up my spine as the curtain blew with the wind. "Has he not had the maids clean all this time?"

I spotted the bird flying into an open room. As I walked in, the bird was perched on the end of a bed. I saw a bunch of people crying and sitting next to the bed. When I walked closer I could see a man lying in the bed. He was pale, no color left in his face. He had a sword laying by his side and was dressed in rags. "Who are you? Why are you in my castle?"

No word came from them. "Why don't you just leave us alone? Time to mourn for our father," a woman said as her hand reached towards the sword.

I just stood there really confused. "Father!" I yelled. "Father, where are you?" The man opened his eyes and quickly grabbed the sword, lunging at me while stabbing me right through the stomach.

I gasped, reaching for the handle of the sword. Crying, I looked up and saw the man's pale face smiling, and his red, blue colored eyes smiling with his grin. "Now die. You don't deserve the throne."

As he pulled the sword out of my stomach I screamed. I used every bit of strength I had to leave the room. I stumbled as I walked. The man was following not saying a word, just smiling and laughing. "Father, where are you? I need your help!" I yelled as I started to get dizzy.

"Your father can't help you, Kia. He's already dead. When I kill you, the Dark Master will become the sole ruler and no one can stop the Dark Master." He started to laugh louder.

"Father. Please help!" I yelled crying and choking on my tears. I reached for my father's bedroom, hoping he was inside. As I pushed the door open I fell to the ground. I stumbled back to my feet. When I looked up I saw my father's body next to his bed. I looked around to see if there was anyone else in his room.

"Father…" I dashed over to him as I started to scream. "Father…No!" He had been decapitated. I turned around and the man was standing in the doorway holding his head.

"I told you he was already dead." As he laughed, it pierced my ears.

"How dare you."

I started to lunge for him with what little strength I had left. He grabbed my throat and lifted me off the ground. "I told you he was dead. Now, why don't you be a good girl and die with him." He dropped my dad's head and picked up a sword. He slowly pushed it into my chest.

I tried to scream, but the pain was too excruciating. I stared into his eyes and watched them change from their red blue color to a solid blue. "You can't be," I choked out

25

the strength to say. I then saw my mother walk around the corner. Her white outfit was giving off a bright glow.

"Taeli ogio fuo yima ruetahogiuade." As she waved her hand in front her she started to glow brighter.

"No, never. She will die!" the man said as he growled.

Mother put her hand on his arm that was holding my neck.

He started to scream, and dropped the sword and me with it. "You will die, I will make sure of it!" He vanished in a cloud of blue and red smoke.

My mother rushed over to me and picked me up. "It will be alright." She took me to my dad's bed and lay me next to his body. "You will be just fine," she said as tears began rolling down her face.

"Mother." I gurgled out the words. I reached to touch her face and as I touched her tears I woke up, screaming. My clothes were covered in blood but there were no stab marks to show how the blood got there. I saw the little fairy who had gotten in the fight with Esom next to me covered in blood as well. She flew up to my face and touched my cheek as I noticed she was crying.

Esom and Grend burst through the door. Starlin woke up and jumped out of bed. "What is going on?" she said franticly.

The fairy flew over to Esom. As she spoke, his face went white.

"No, how could the Shades have gotten in here?"

"What is it?" I said.

"The Shades tried to kill you but your mother saved your life."

"My mother?"

"Yes, she is here. She saved your life."

"How? My mother died when I was young," I said angrily.

"This fairy here is your mother."

"How can this be?"

As I stood up I was getting dizzy. I stumbled over to Esom and grabbed him by his shirt. I went to punch him in his face when the fairy flew between us. She looked as though she was in a great deal of pain. She placed her tiny hand on my forehead and started to speak. At first I could not understand her then I started to make out what she was saying.

"Eseialipo Kia netasili ota ema…Don't ebu deama taa maiho tai sei…not his taliuafu…it might be deruaho to understand at first, but it is true I am your mother. Kia, you have grown up so strong and beautiful. I have saved your life by letting the Shade take mine. You are wondering how I am still alive after you watched me die so many years ago."

As she was talking I started to cry. I could hear her voice as it was when I was a child. I was in shock that I could see my mother again. Even though I was very confused regarding how she was a fairy, I started to see images of what she was talking about.

"Kia, when the Kings and Queens of our planet die they do not return to the planet like all living creatures do. When the Kings and Queens die, their souls are reborn as a fairy. For it was a spell that the first Queen cast as she was dying. She wanted to preserve the knowledge of our past and keep it alive. Before her there were no such thing as fairies, with her spell she wanted to create a new life and one that could be one with the planet. *cough, cough, cough.* Preserve the life, and keep all knowledge safe. This land we are in is not known to many. We cannot leave the forest, if we do we will permanently die."

"How did you save my life?"

27

cough, cough, cough, cough "Do you remember in your dream when that man stabbed you in your stomach and your chest?"

"Yes."

"Well, each fairy is given a gift and we do not know what that gift is until it is time to use it. Mine was protection."

"Protection? What do you mean?"

"The Shades as you know are very powerful, they can enter dreams and kill you if they desire to, but only as a last resort. When you were stabbed, and after the Shade left, I picked you up to put you on the bed. When you touched my tears your wounds were transferred from you to me."

She fell to the floor, I could no longer hear her voice. "What do you mean?"

Esom slowly bent down and gently picked her up. He walked over to the bed and placed her on the pillow. Fairies started to fly into the room and surround the bed. "What is going on?"

Starlin walked over to me and held my hand.

"She is dying, Kia," Esom said concerned. "She told you how." His voice went stern.

"But why? I can't lose my mother again." I started to cry.

She started to speak again, I was not able to hear her, though I so desperately wished that I could. I walked over to her and placed my hand as close as I could without touching her, for I was afraid of hurting her even more. She placed her tiny hand on mine.

Esom started to speak for her. "I am leaving you again. I am so sorry that I cannot stay with you. Even though I am not going to be with you, remember I will always be with you."

Her grip started to loosen.

"Mother. No, I can't let you go."

"O evaioli uoyi." Her eyes started to close and the fairies were moving closer towards her. Her body was glowing and getting brighter by the second. Esom helped me up and moved me away from the bed. I was fighting him the whole time, I did not want to be away from her. I wanted to be right by her side. The room started to get really bright and I could not see anything. "Mother!"

The light faded and as it did, I saw a cloud of dust that shimmered in the light. Esom let me go and I ran over to the bed. She was gone, the fairies were catching the shimmering dust that was in the air. Another fairy flew into the room with a tiny bottle tied to a piece of leather. One by one the fairies placed the dust into the bottle. When all the dust had been collected, they placed it around my neck.

Another fairy started to speak, and Esom translated. "Let her light protect you." Then he flew out the window and the rest of the fairies followed. I went over to the bed and placed my hand where she once laid. I clenched the bottle around my neck. "Mother, why did I have to lose you twice?"

"I know it's not easy losing a parent. I know how you feel but I cannot imagine what it feels like to lose a parent twice. Kia, things will get better. Just remember what she said, 'Even though I am not going to be with you, remember I will always be with you.' Remember we still have to go to your father. You cannot let this get to you."

"You're right," I growled. "I will take my revenge on the Shades and make them pay for me losing my mother again."

"But you don't even know where they are?" Grend said.

"No, but if they are after me I can find them. Let's get going to my father's." I stood up from the bed and as I did I started to get dizzy. I was losing my balance and my vision was getting blurry.

Esom ran over to me to catch me from falling. "It's time for some rest." Esom's eyes were solid red as he kissed me slightly on my forehead.

Esom picked me up and placed me on the bed. Starlin and Grend slowly walked out of the room. Grend stopped, turned around and watched Esom while he lay me down. "You coming?" Grend said crestfallen.

"No, I'm going to stay here with her. We have already caused her so much pain it's the least I can do," Esom said sadly.

And without a word, Grend slowly closed the door.

Chapter Seven

Starlin and Grend walked down the hallway. Grend looked towards Starlin and he is finally able to see the pain on her face of what had just happened. He didn't say a word to her, as they came to the end of the hallway Starlin stopped and fell to her knees. He was able to tell that she was crying but trying very hard to hold back her tears. He reached down to touch her shoulder to help console her.

"Don't touch me," an irate Starlin sounded as she looked at Grend and pushed his hand off her.

She stood up and walked down the hallway. Grend was shocked that she pushed his hand away, but at the same time he was happy that she still had her fighting spirit. He followed her to the dining hall. She sat down in a chair as a fairy brought her a glass of white angel flower tea. "Thank you." As she smiled, the male fairy nodded to her and flew off bumping into Grend.

"Why are you following me?" she snapped at him.

"The Shades are out there and I need to protect you."

"I don't need protecting," she said still grousing.

"You need more protecting than you think," he said sits next to her.

She stood up and walked over to the window. While leaning over the window sill to see farther out Grend approached her. "You know you shouldn't be so locked up?"

"Why? Be open like Kia and let my emotions get the best of me?" Starlin started to get mad as she turned her head and gazed off into the distance.

"Want to tell me about it?"

"Tell you about what?"

"How you are feeling right now?"

"What! No, I don't even know you. What makes you think I want to share anything with you?"

"To let it out."

Angrily, Starlin spun around and pushed Grend out of her way and stormed off. When she reached the door she went to push it open when she got a a flash of her family happy and everyone sitting at the dining table eating. She stopped and a tear ran down her cheek. She shook her head and wiped it away.

As she opened the door she was shocked by what was in the room. Wall to wall, floor to ceiling covered in books. Grend finished pushing the door open for her.

"What is all this?"

"The history of our planet and all the knowledge from our Kings and Queens." He reached for a book to show her what he was talking about. A female fairy came out of nowhere and grabbed the book from his hand and started yelling at him.

"Uoyi taonanaki chuota eseihota seikiobu. Yilinao ehota Neeqe dena Kiben naki. Ogi yiawia uoyi erua tanona demaokiliewi erueho."

"What is she saying?"

"I don't know." Disappointed sounding.

"You don't know. How can Esom understand them and you can't?"

"He grew up here I didn't"

"He did?"

Grend quickly grabbed Starlin's hand and dragged her to a table in the middle of room. It has a glass lid and a map inside the case. "Let go." As she tried to pull her hand away she looked into Grend's eyes and they were glazed over as he was staring deeply into the glass casing. "Let go."

She punched him in the nose which made him bleed. When the blood dripped off his face, a drop landed on the glass, and he let go of her hand. The glass slowly moved up and looked as though it had wrapped itself onto the bottom of the table. When the case opened fully, the map was gone, and in its place was a pile of white angel flowers.

"What is with the flowers?"

His eyes were no longer glazed over, and he looked confused. "I don't know, I've never seen this before. I didn't even think this could open. Where did the map go? I wanted to show you where I grew up."

"Why? I don't like you. Why are you wanting to get so close to me?"

When Grend was about to speak, a small green light started to shine in the flowers. The light was rising and glowing brighter. It moved towards Grend and turned blue, the light then moved towards Starlin while slowly turning white. As the light moved closer to her chest the glow got brighter until it formed a white angel flower necklace around her neck.

"What is this?" Starlin asked as she picked up the pendant around her neck.

"I don't know, but it suits you." His eyes were glazed over again, he had a devilish smile on his face as he picked up her hand and kissed it. She started to close her eyes and got weak in the knees, and as she was falling backwards Grend quickly reaches for her. He caught her and brought her over to a bench. After laying her down he got up and walked over to a fountain hiding behind one of the bookshelves.

When he sat down on the fountain he looked towards Starlin to see little girl standing by her side. Her hair was long almost to the ground, red and curly. She had a spiky tail and her clothes were black as night. The girl turned around and glared at him while shaking her head. She pointed towards a bookshelf while walking over to it as if wanting him to follow. Curious about her, he stood up and followed her to the bookshelf.

She pointed out a book, and when Grend reached for the book it moved on its own and then fell off the shelf. As soon as it hit the floor the bookshelf moved forwards a little bit and opened to reveal a passage covered in black angel flowers.

The little girl looked behind her and pointed to Starlin. Even though she was not saying a word he knew what she wanted him to do. He walked over to Starlin, picked her up and started to carry her down the passage. As soon as he entered the passage the bookshelf closed behind them. When it went pitch black he felt a tug on his shirt. He saw the little girl's tail start to glow red starting from the tip and moving towards her body. Once her tail was fully bright the passage lit up with red light. She pointed down the passage and starred to walk.

After some time of walking, he wondered if the passage was ever going to end. As it twisted and turned, he finally saw a light coming through a crack in the wall. He used his shoulder to push the wall open. The light coming from the open wall blinded him, but after his vision adjusted to the light he noticed white and black angel flowers growing on vines up the wall and even on the chandelier hanging above a glowing red fountain.

The fountain was made of red marble and carved with Skins and Scales. Some were holding each other while others looked like the Scales were chasing the Skins which had the look of fear on their faces. He could see sunlight through openings in the ceiling.

The little girl walked over to the fountain and got in the water. She started to sink and slowly vanished under.

Even though she had not said a word, he put Starlin in the water. As soon as Starlin was completely submerged she sat up gasping for air.

"What the hell, trying to drown me?"

Once she saw her surrounding she asked, "How did we get here?"

Grend didn't say a word because when he was about to the little girl who led them there showed up, standing in front of Starlin outside the fountain smiling.

"Who is this?"

"I don't know, she just showed up and led us here. I've never seen her before."

Starlin stood up then got out of the fountain. The little girl walked over to her and touched her arm. In an instant, she was dry. "My name is Dresia." Right after her name was said she vanished in a cloud of red smoke

Chapter Eight

"What now?" she demanded, glaring at him. "I don't see any way out of here."

"I came in from that direction." As he turned around the door they came through was gone.

"Oh, you mean that door? You're right. let's get going." The tone was sarcastic.

"It doesn't look like there is a door anywhere. I only see the light shining through the ceiling and these holes are way too tiny for us to fit through."

"We need to find a way out."

Grend walked towards the wall seeing if he could feel for another door. Starlin went over to the other side and started doing the same thing. After what felt like forever of searching, the fountain and the chandelier started to vanish.

"What's going on, Grend? What did you touch?"

"Nothing, I swear." He backed away from the wall. As the ground started to shake the light coming from the ceiling started to get covered by the black angel flowers making it very hard to see. When the ground stopped shaking there was only one hole in the ceiling that had very little light shining through.

Starlin and Grend walked over to the light.

"Do you notice that?

"Notice what? That you caused all the light to go out and got us stuck in this damn room?" she snapped at Grend.

"No, look at the light."

"You know we wouldn't have to be in here if you didn't kiss my hand." Her temper was rising. "It's all your fault."

"My fault, if you didn't irritate the hell out of me I

wouldn't have kissed your hand in the first place." His voice was getting louder and more aggressive.

"My fault?" She started to get closer to Grend.

"You're an emotionless prick. You are all mister high and mighty thinking you can tell me what to do. Well, I got news for you. You're not my father." She was now yelling right in his face.

They were so close to each other they could feel their body heat emitting off one another. Starlin punched Grend directly in the chest, which forced him to step back two feet from her. "How dare you." His tone was deep and his eyes were piercing staring straight at her.

As he made a fist she said, "You wouldn't hit a girl would you?" trying to sound innocent and pretending she was a child.

"You're not a girl." Her expression changed as she was clenching her jaw.

He swung his fist towards her and as she dodged it she quipped, "Is that all you got? You fought a lot better when I was a child," taunting him while smirking.

He threw another punch but as she went to dodge it he kneed her in the chest. As the force was pulling her backwards she quickly grabbed his waist and threw him onto the ground while punching him in the ribs.

"Are you ever going to let me in?" He rolled her over while putting her in an arm lock.

"Ugh… Never…. You are not worth letting in." She relaxed enough to let him know he won. She stood up rubbing her arm and walked over to the light and stared. He walked over next to her when she turned around and then went over to the wall in a huff, doing everything she can to get away from him.

She paced around the room while holding her hand out and lightly brushing the flowers. One of the black angel flowers fell and landed on her foot. She bent down to pick it up, and as she did the black angel flower pricked her finger. She let go and as she watched it fall a single drop of blood from her finger followed the flower. As it touched the floor, her drop of blood landed in the center of the flower turning it white.

"What on earth?" Scared, she started taking a couple of steps back away from the flower.

Grend walked over to her to see what she was looking at. Every black angel flower was turning white. It soon quickly spread across the floor, up the walls and then on the ceiling. Dresia appeared again, this time she was hanging from the ceiling where the light was still shining through. Her laughter was echoing throughout the room.

Dresia's tail glowed a brighter red. She slowly lowered herself down with the use of her tail. When her feet touched the ground, she was holding the last black angel flower while watching it turn white.

Where the color changes had begun, the flowers started to wither and turn to dust, this time quicker than the color change. The only one that did not was the one Dresia was holding. The dust started to form piles on the floor as the fountain and chandelier slowly reappeared. The dust on the floor began to swirl and the fountain started to glow.

Dresia smiled as her laughter stopped. "You're mine now." The dust swirled around Dresia as they watched her and the dust disappear.

"What just happened?"

"No idea. I still blame you, Grend. You got us into this." Angry, she said, "I can't move."

Chapter Nine

Starlin's eyes started to glow white as her gaze was caught in the glow of the fountain. The white emitting from her eyes spread to fill the whole room. When the brightness faded she was back in the village where she grew up.

Starlin looked around and noticed nothing had changed. Her heart started to race as she saw her brother running towards her father. Her father looked over to her and gestured for her to come to him with a smile. She began to run towards him and tripped on a rock while landing in a puddle of water. She stared at her reflection; her face was young, her eyes innocent and her freckles more prominent. All that was on her mind was her father reaching out for her. She rubbed the mud from her mouth as she got up and continued to run towards him.

"Your mother has been worried sick about you two. With the increase in Shades you know it's not safe to be out by your selves."

"Sorry, Papa. It won't happen again. We were just playing hide and seek," Starlin's brother said.

"Well let's go home. Your mother is just about done with dinner."

They walked into their home, the single roomed house was filled with art and pottery of white angel flowers. There was only one window and a small fireplace where her mother was making dinner and wiping her hands on her apron.

"When are we going to sell all of this art and pottery Starlin has made? Get it out of here and give us more room?" her brother said nagging his dad as he elbowed Starlin with a smile.

"I'm not sure. Your sister has never seen a white angel flower. Well as a matter of fact none of us ever have. We are not even sure if this is really what they look like."

"Father, enough talk of selling her art. She is only eight years old and look at the marvel she has created. Maybe one day she will make art for the King and Queen," her mother said as she filled up bowls with the soup from the kettle.

Later that night after they had all gone to bed Starlin was determined to find a white angel flower so they could sell her art and pottery to be able to a live a more lavish lifestyle. She gathered some of the leftover bread and her hooded cloak and snuck out the window. She headed to the edge of town when she saw a white light appearing in the woods. Her curiosity piqued as she walked towards the light. It moved and Starlin giggled, she followed the light for what seemed like hours when just as it appeared it vanished.

When she looked around to see where it had gone she noticed she was standing in a field of white angel flowers. She picked the only one that was shining in a single ray of moonlight, for that was all that she needed as proof. Even though she had no idea where she was, she knew the exact way home as if something was telling her which way to go.

As she got closer to home she could hear screaming and the smell of smoke. She dropped the flower, and in a dead run headed for home. The closer she got the more she could see. There were Shades everywhere killing everyone in the village. She could hear the Shades asking people before they killed them, "Where is it?"

When she got to her house it was engulfed in flames. She could hear her family screaming. There was no way out. The door was blocked and half of the house had already caved in. Starlin franticly searched for a way in but she could not find one. The cries from her family suddenly stopped, and she saw a Shade walking around a house as if looking for someone.

She didn't want to die too so she ran as fast and as far as she could. She made it to a lake somewhere outside and far from her village. The sun was just rising when she fell asleep. When the sun was high she woke up crying. She was there for what seemed like days when a girl came up to her and asked what was wrong. The little girl told her that her name was Kia.

Starlin started to get surrounded by white light again. It got so bright it hurt her eyes, and when the light subsided she was back in the room with Grend crying. She fell to the floor and wiped her face with her arm. "We need to get out of here."

"That's what I've been trying to tell you. Will you look at the light?" He pretended not to care that she was crying or what just happened to her. Starlin looked towards the light and now that the flowers were gone she could see shadows moving across the light as if they were just underneath another room.

Chapter Ten

As Starlin followed a shadow, she noticed a hole in the floor that was the same shape as her pendant. She took off the pendant hoping that it would fit. As she got closer to placing it into the hole, a red light started to shine and surround the pendant as it hovered just slightly above the hole. The room started to shake again, this time the door that they came through began to re-appear and slowly open.

"Let's get out of here," Starlin said, and as she reached to grab the pendant it shocked her.

"Leave it."

She tried to pick it up one more time, it shocked her again. "Ouch!" she yelped as she put her finger in her mouth to sooth the pain emitting from the shock. Her and Grend left the room and walked down the long and pitch black path, with only the feel of the wall under their hands to find their way out for the hallway's twists and turns.

"Finally, we are out of that room. If I ever pass out again because of you. Don't touch me ever!" she snarled while pushing Grend out of her way.

Starlin walked over to the window again and stared out as if lost in thought.

Grend wanted to see if he could get her to talk to him. He started to walk over to her when he stopped and just stared instead, wondering what she was thinking about, even though he had a very good idea.

As the day went on, Starlin stared out the window not moving at all. As the sun started to set she turned around with a smile on her face.

"You've been here the whole time? I thought you had left?"

"I have been just standing here watching you."

"That was creepy sounding. You sound like a stalker." She giggled. Her laugh startled her. She had not laughed in a long time.

"That was different for you. Are you sure you are ok?"

"Yes, I am fine. I want to go back to Kia and see how she is doing."

She walked past Grend as he followed keeping his distance. Starlin pounded on the door like she did back at Kia's cottage. As she opened the door it hit Esom who was reaching for the door. "Sorry." She walked past Esom and over to Kia. As she sat on the bed Kia rolled over and pushed her off.

"What was that for?" As she stood up about to pounce on her she noticed she was still sleeping. "How long is she going to sleep?" she said concerned.

"I'm not sure. We do need to get going soon. When she wakes up this time I am hoping she is well enough so that way we can be on our way."

#######

A couple of days had gone by, Esom never left her side. Grend would bring him food but he never touched it and left it on the table by the bed. This time when Grend was bringing Esom another plate of food, as he knocked on the door like he always had this time Kia opened the door with a smile. "Thank you, Grend," she said as she grabbed the food from him and walked over to a table by the fireplace. "I'm starving," she said as she dug into the food.

"How long has she been awake for?"

"About half of the day. She doesn't remember much of what has happened."

"Why didn't you come get us? What does she

remember?"

"I told him not to, I wanted to be with just Esom for a little bit longer. Let's see, I remember Starlin busting into my house, almost getting me killed, running into you two. Waking up in a cave, ending up in Ethorn and finding out my mother was still alive. Then the last thing I remember is her dying again." Picking up the soup bowl she drank right out of it instead of using the spoon.

"You don't remember how or why she died this time?"

"Nope, and I would prefer if you didn't tell me. I don't think I could handle the pain again," she said as she shoved bread in her mouth.

Starlin came into the room to see what all the commotion was about. "Kia!" Starlin ran over to her and gave her a hug.

Kia said, "Nice to see you too," with her mouth full of food.

"You ready to get going back to your father's?" Starlin asked her with a big smile.

"Yes, when can we get going, Esom?"

"Tomorrow, it's getting dark outside and we need to get provisions before we leave. We have a long road ahead of us."

"Starlin, will you stay with her tonight? Grend and I will get things prepared for tomorrow."

"Of course, you don't even have to ask me that."

As Grend and Esom left the room, Starlin sat next to Kia childish like and bouncing up and down. "So, what was it like?"

"What are you talking about? Are you ok, you are acting strange, Starlin."

"Yes, I am fine, I am just wondering what it is like to be alone with a hunk like that."

"Ok, now I know something is wrong. You never

talk like that," Kia said as she put her hands on her shoulder, seeing if she could look into her eyes.

Starlin thought for a second. "You know you're right. I never had, huh. That's odd of me." She started to laugh.

"There is something different about you, but I can't put my finger on it." She let go of her.

"Well, let's not worry about it and just get some sleep."

Starlin walked over to the bed and flopped down. Patting the bed, she gestured to Kia to come join her. Smiling, Kia ran over to the bed and jumped on it which made Starlin bounce a little on the bed. Starlin picked up a pillow and hit Kia with it. "Pillow fight!" Kia reached for another pillow. Later, Esom and Grend walked into the room to find feathers all over the place and both of them asleep on the floor next to the fireplace.

"What happened here?"

"No idea. Though it reminds me of when we found them in the great hall at the castle in the same situation." Esom grabbed the door to close it again.

"Esom," he said as they walked out of the room. "Do you think we have a chance of getting back to the King?"

"We should, I am hoping the Dark Master doesn't interfere too much. We really need to get her back and make sure nothing happens to her."

Kia woke up to the sound of dripping water on the window. She sat up and looked around. "Starlin, wake up." Kia poked her several times. "As usual you don't ever want to wake up." Kia stood up, grabbed the last pillow that had very little feathers in it and hit Starlin as hard as she could.

"OK. OK. I'm up," she said, rubbing her eyes and spitting feathers out of her mouth.

"Let's go look for Esom and Grend so we can get back on our way home."

Kia and Starlin walked out of their room and bumped into Grend and Esom who were standing outside of the door quietly talking to one another.

"Oh, you're up? Shall we get going? We have everything we need to be able to make it back to the King."

Outside, the sun was coming up over the treetops, and four horses were waiting for them. Esom helped Kia up onto her horse and Grend helped Starlin. Kia watched them and as she noticed Starlin smiling at Grend, she quietly said, "I know something is wrong with her." After they were all on their horses a fairy flew up to Esom.

"What is he saying?"

"Nothing, it's none of your concern."

Chapter Eleven

She didn't think twice on it. "What woods are we in? I do not recognize what forest this is, I have never seen some of these plants before."

"It's called Sapphire Woods."

"I have never heard of it."

Starlin started to giggle. When I looked over at her I saw Grend had just whispered something into her ear. Which I could only assume was why she was laughing. It was strange to see Starlin so happy and carefree. She was a completely different person from how I knew her. I tried to push how strange she was acting out of my head and focus on what lay ahead of us. It was hard for me to do, but I was finally able to manage it and focus on our journey ahead. We started heading into the woods farther. The Sapphire Woods were thick, the grass was tall and soft as it was when I first entered Ethorn.

The path was very narrow, we had to form a single line in order to stay on the path so our horses did not have to walk on the tall crystals that lined it. The Sapphire Woods had a very sweet smell to them, I was not sure why that was but it was quite soothing. The forest was lined with blue flowers, blue rocks and even the trees had a blue tint to them.

As time went on Starlin kept looking back towards Grend and smiling, every time she did she would blush. When the path widened, it was just a little bigger and we could have two horses side by side. Starlin moved back towards Grend, they made sure to ride a little way behind us as to not let Esom and I see what they were doing. I could not hear what they were saying but whatever they were talking about they seemed to be enjoying each other's company.

Nightfall was upon us on our first day into the woods, and the smell that was sweet where we entered the forest was dissipating. As the sun was setting the sky was turning different shades of orange and red which made the light shining on the trees turn purple. The light slowly vanished behind the trees as the rocks all over the forest started to glow. It was mystifying, as I looked around I did not see many creatures. As a matter of fact, I did not see anything not even a bug.

"Why are there no bugs or anything in these woods?"

"They hide during the night," Esom creepily said.

"Why is that?"

"No one knows. There are rumors of a creature in these woods that they say is so tall and massive that just to look at it turns you to stone."

"What?" Starlin gasped and grabbed hold of Grend's hand.

"Yes, we just have to make sure we do not run into that creature."

"Why does it only come out at night?" I wondered.

"That is a question no one knows the answer to."

Just as Esom spoke a tree in the distance fell and Starlin and I both jumped. "What was that?" I softly said to myself. I quickly and tightly grabbed the reins of my horse. The wind started to pick up and it was getting cold. Esom looked over to me, took a blanket from his satchel and put it around me. I blushed when I felt his touch on me. I looked behind me and saw Starlin off her horse and on Grend's wrapped in a blanket.

"When did she get onto his horse? We never stopped. What is wrong with her? She has never acted this way in her life. Not even towards me; she hated anyone touching her, unless she touched them first. As a matter of fact, she has been acting strange ever since my mother died …… again," I said as I looked off into the distance.

"I know what you mean, Grend does not like anyone either. He might seem concerned about others but deep down he only cared for himself. Something has gotten into both of them and I do not like it at all."

"Do you think we should find a place to rest for the night?"

"No, you do not want to stop in the woods at night. It is said terrible things can happen in these woods at night. We must keep traveling till daybreak. Then we can rest."

"Is it because of the creature that lives here?"

"No idea." Esom started to laugh.

"What is so funny?"

"You should see the look on your face."

"Why? Do I have something on it?"

He started to laugh harder. "No. There is no such thing as a creature in these woods, and we can stop at any time we like." He stopped his horse and dismounted. "You really believed me? That's hilarious."

"You… You…" I started to clench my fists.

"Let me help you down." He walked over to help me down.

"Don't, I might be a princess but I don't need your help."

"Grend, let's go." As he looked back, Starlin and Grend were kissing. "Grend!" he admonished, snapping at him.

"What?"

"What the hell are you doing? You know your kiss will make her fall asleep." As Esom looked down at Starlin he noticed she was not asleep but wide awake.

"What the hell? Why are you not sleeping? What is going on with you two?" Esom was shocked and mad at the same time.

"Starlin? Are you ok? What is wrong with you?" I sounded concerned.

"Grend, let's get going to your place now! I would like to have a talk with you."

"What, he lives around here? I thought he lived with you?" I looked confused.

"No, these woods are my home. This is where I grew up before I became a guard to the royal family. We still have a long way to go before we reach the house I grew up in."

"Grend, I would like to talk to you. Now!"

Grend and Esom walked off out of sight leaving Starlin and I alone with the horses. I dismounted my horse, walked over to her and stared at her. While staring at her eyes I noticed they were glazed over, her cheeks were flushed, she was smirking and her lips were moving slightly as if she was talking but there was no sound. "Starlin, are you ok?" I touched her leg and she jumped. Her eyes were no longer glazed, her cheeks were no longer flushed and her smirk was gone.

"Yes, Kia?" She sounded startled, as if I never asked if she was ok to begin with.

"I said are you ok?"

"Yes, why do you ask?"

"You have been acting strange ever since we were in Ethorn."

"Yes, I am fine, I have never been better."

I let go of her leg and she dismounted. "Where are the other two?"

"You don't remember, we just saw them walk off."

"No, I didn't even know we had stopped." As I

looked around the forest I did not see anything or anyone. We tied the horses to a tree, and walked in the direction Esom and Grend walked off in. As the wind was blowing it was getting colder and stronger; I wrapped my blanket around me tighter. I stopped and turned around to see if Starlin was still following. She was stopped and staring at the night sky. "Starlin, are you coming?"

Starlin looked at me and smiled. "Yes, sorry. The sky is really beautiful tonight." She walked towards me and I got the feeling that something was watching us. The farther we got into the woods and away from the path the brighter the crystals' glow was and the colder it was getting.

The wind was blowing extremely hard, and I started to see snow falling. When I looked closer at the snow, I noticed it was not white snow. The snow was blue and shimmering in the moonlight, just like the glow of the crystals. I looked up thinking the sky was going to be cloudy and dark and that we should get to shelter, but to my surprise when I looked up the sky was clear. Even with the wind, the trees were not swaying.

I looked towards Starlin and saw that she had a smile on her face and was trying to catch the blue snowflakes on her tongue. With each snowflake she caught I started to see a blue shimmer in her eyes. It was as though the more she caught the more her eyes would sparkle. Starlin picked up some snow off the ground. When I wasn't looking, she threw it at me and hit my arm. I turned around and right when I was about to get mad at her she threw another one and this time it hit my face. I started to laugh very hard. "No, you didn't." I grabbed some snow myself and started to throw it back at her. Next thing I know we were having a huge snowball fight.

In the distance, something watched us curiously,

it seemed, as it tilted its head from side to side. The trees moved and creaked as if they were about to break as the creature watched. We did not notice as the creature moved closer and closer. It remained in the tall shadows of the trees as not to be seen. With a slight movement from the creature a tree branch fell. This was not just a small branch either, it sounded as though half of a tree had fallen over. We stopped laughing and looked in the direction of the fallen branch.

Chapter Twelve

Esom and Grend came to a stop at the only brown with green tint tree in the forest. When Grend reached to put his hand on the tree, Esom grabbed his hand and stopped him.

"Explain to me how now your kiss no longer works on her?"

"I don't know. I thought for sure that if I was to kiss her again she would fall asleep. I am tired of her and her laughter. With her smile that just tantalizes me to kiss her, and her eyes glimmer with an irritating glow that I cannot look away from. I thought that if I kissed her I wouldn't have to see it anymore."

"How can you say that? You have been acting like you are in love with her."

"Are you nuts?" Angry, Grend balled his fist up. "I wanted nothing to do with her. I figured that if I played along she would follow more easily. Before we left she didn't want to go, it was not until I started to pretend I cared for her that she started following us, and that kept us moving."

"So, you don't love her?"

"No, I do not. I want nothing to do with her."

"You have no idea why your kiss no longer works on her?"

"No, ever since," he placed his hand on the tree, "we came out of that room she has been acting strange."

"What room?"

"The one in the library." The tree glowed green, bark collapsed in on itself and a lever appeared. Grend placed his hand on the lever and pulled.

"There is no room in there. There are just books."

"Well we found one, and ever since she has been

acting strange."

Grend pulled the lever down, the ground started to shake but only slightly. Around them the trees shook, the wind blew harder, and blue snow started to fall. There was now a hole in the ground around the bottom of the tree with stairs that led down into the ground.

"Why are we here? This is not your house."

"I need to grab something from my vault."

"I'll be here waiting. Hurry, we don't have much time before 'IT' comes out."

Chapter Thirteen

"What was that?" I said as I grabbed ahold of Starlin's hand.

"No idea. I don't want to stick around and find out though."

The creature in the tree hopped from the tree and on onto another tree. Another branch fell, this time it was closer to the ground. My grip got tighter around Starlin's hand, I took a step back as if I was going to run. The creature jumped from the tree it was sitting in down to the ground will a loud thud. The ground shook as the wind stopped blowing. Even though still in the shadows, I could see the creature's shape. It stood as tall as Starlin, its body was skinny, and I saw what looked like horns on its head. The eyes glowed green. I saw what looked like breathing as a puff of fire sparked around it with each breath.

Just as we were about to run all the snow started to swirl around the creature. It was so thick we no longer could see its shape. Once the swirling snow had stopped the creature was gone, so was the wind and all the snow.

"What was that?" Starlin asked looking towards me as if she was about to cry.

"I have no idea, I do not want to stand around and find out. We need to find the two boys who left us."

We started to head back towards the horses thinking maybe Esom and Grend had gone back there to get us. As we walked back in the direction of the horses I started to hear sounds in the trees. It was almost as if once the creature left bugs appeared in the woods. I was scared and did not want to stick around and find out what that creature was; we walked faster. Finally, we get back to the horses, but Esom and Grend were still not there. I got up onto my horse and wrapped the blanket tighter around me. Starlin sat on the dirt road and started to draw in the dirt with a stick.

"What are you doing, Starlin? I take it you are bored?"

"Just a little, I miss Grend."

"What do you mean. 'Miss Grend?'"

"Nothing, you wouldn't understand," she said with a sigh.

Starlin never liked talking about her feelings so I didn't want to push it any. Starlin stood up walked over to the horse she was riding, grabbed a blanket then sat back where she was on the ground and continued to draw in the dirt. I was confused by how she was acting completely different but then sometimes she acted like herself.

"It does not look like the boys are coming back anytime soon. Do you want to set camp or continue to your father's without them?" Starlin asked me in a concerned way.

"I think we should wait until they get back. Even though that is a great idea to leave them and continue. I do not think we should," I said as I looked off into the woods.

"Well how much longer do you want to wait? I know I do not want to be here all night. I would like to get out of this forest before that thing comes back."

"What do you think it could be?"

"I have no idea but I do not want to stick around and find out."

Snapping at me, she stood up and threw the stick into the woods as if she throwing a dagger. I watched it plunged itself into the tree.

"Wow, how did you do that? I didn't know

you were able to throw like that."

"Grend taught me while you were taking a nap." Starlin turned around and glared at me.

Just when she took a few steps towards me with her hands in a fist I thought she was going to punch me when Esom and Grend walked out of the woods. Esom seemed concerned by something.

"May we keep going?" Grend said as he approached Starlin. He stared at her eyes and seemed concerned.

"Where are we going?" I asked.

"Remember, to my house."

Grend helped Starlin onto her horse as Esom got onto his. Grend guided his horse in front of Esom's and mine as Starlin followed. Once they were a few feet ahead of us we started to follow. Even though it was night I was the only one who seemed to be very cold. I was shivering under the blanket I had I on. Esom saw I was shivering and placed another blanket on me.

"Thank you."

He just smiled.

"How far is it to Grend's house?"

"Not far. We are close."

"I would like to get out of this cold and be by a nice warm fire eating some sort of food."

"Don't worry, maybe a few hours and we will be there."

"What do you mean maybe a few hours?"

"I have only been to his place a few times and do not remember how long it takes to get there."

"I see, where did you two go?"

"We went to talk."

"What about?"

"That is of none of your concern."

As we traveled, the road got wider and the trees got bigger. The sweet smell that I noticed when I first entered the forest started to return. It felt like we had been traveling for hours. Grend stopped and get off his horse. "Take the bags from the horses. We must walk from here." He took the bags from his horse and then pushed the horse away. We all got off our horses and pushed them away as well.

"Why did we just do that?"

"They cannot go where we are going from here. It is too dangerous for them."

"By any chance where are we going from here?"

"This way."

He walked off into the woods, and we all followed. The trees were thick, there was no grass on the ground just dirt and large roots that intertwined into one another. Even though the trees were thick, however you could still see the moon's light shining through the canopy.

Chapter Fourteen

The horses were spooked, and the ground shook which made one of the horses fall over. A large tail moved from out of the shadows and grabbed the horse that fell over by its hind legs. It moved the horse close to its face and smelled the saddle, with a deep breath the hair on the horse was drawn into the nose of the creature. The creature sneezed as it dropped the horse. With another deep breath it looks in the direction we traveled.

A distorted mysterious voice echoed. "Get them. Now."

########

As we walked the ground was more rocks and roots, the canopy got thinner and the ground was now at a upwards slant as if we were heading up a hill. The climb got harder as the ground got rockier and less roots were showing.

"Where are we?" I said, exhausted. No one answered me, they just keep walking. The hill got steeper and the rocks bigger. "Your house is all the way up here?" Still no one answered me.

Starlin tripped on a rock. Grend was standing right next to her and with quick action he reached down and grabbed her hand before she hit the ground. As he pulled her up she was blushing and slightly smiling. They didn't say a word, just smiled at each other. A little further up he stopped at a flat spot on the rocks.

"We will stop here for the rest of the night."

"I thought you said that we couldn't stay in the forest at night?" Starlin said.

"Yes, I did, but that was down there in the forest, up here we are just fine. Let's make a fire and get something to eat."

As we sat around the fire I stared at the sky watching the stars. My mind started to wander on how my father was doing, will he be ok and will I be able to make it in time before he dies? I was not sure if I was even ready to become queen. I left because I didn't want to become queen, it reminded me too much of my mother. I didn't think I can ever live up to her name. She was such a role model for many and always knew how to talk to me to help me figure things out. I wished my mother was still here. I hid a tear that ran down my cheek as I grasped the necklace of my mother around my neck.

"What are you thinking about?" Esom sat next to me.

"Nothing." I turned away and looked towards the moon.

"You sure? You notice that it's a full a moon tonight?"

"Yes, I do see that. What is your point?" I asked as I turned away from him.

"You can show me how you fly if you like? Just to take your mind off of whatever it is you are thinking about." He took my hand.

I looked at his hand then moved my gaze to his eyes as I watched them changing colors to a solid red. He helped me stand up and we both walked away from Grend and Starlin. He took me to an area where we could no longer see either of them or the glow of the fire.

"Do you want to show me now?" He grabbed my hand.

"I don't know. I am kind of embarrassed by it."

"Why? You have no need to by shy." As he

took off his coat and extended his wings, he added, "I will go with you."

I grabbed the amulet from out of my pocket and put it around my neck. It started to glow, and as I closed my eyes wings appeared on my back. My wings sparkled like the forest did and was glowing blue with green sparkling light. He took my hand again and lifted himself off the ground with his powerful wings. "I have only flown a few times, even though I was taught when I was younger I have forgotten how to use them." He looked at me with his red eyes and taught again, me how to use my wings.

After a few minutes of him teaching me, I started to remember how to keep my balance and fly at the same time. He let go of my hand, and as I fell a little bit, he quickly tried to catch me when I got my balance. I smiled "I am fine, I think I got the hang of it now." We flew higher in the moon-light, and it looked as though we are dancing with one other. My necklace that I had around my neck that was given to me by the fairies started to glow a soft white.

"What is happening? I didn't know it glowed."

"You don't remember?"

"Remember what?" As we stopped I pulled my hand away.

"Never mind, I hope you remember soon."

"Remember what?"

"It is not my place to say. You need to remember things on your own or the memory of it will be corrupted and will not be your true memory."

"So, I only remember this necklace from my mother, but I don't remember why I have it but in time I will?"

"Yes, I hope that time is soon. Losing your

memories can be painful, for you do not know them."

"Well I would still have my memories if you didn't take them from me."

"How would I take your memories? I cannot do that."

"Yes, you can. When you kiss me, Starlin told me that sometimes the kiss can cause memory loss."

"Yes, that is true and I am sorry that I have kissed you. I have only been trying to protect you."

"Protect me? Protect me from what?"

"Making choices that can put you in more danger."

"Well that is my choice to make. Not yours."

Esom's eyes started to turn blue. "You will not make it to your father," he said as reached for the amulet around my neck.

"What are you doing?" I moved away from him. "You know if I do not have this I cannot fly."

"That is the point," he said as he grabbed for it again.

I quickly headed for the ground. He was right behind me growling as he flew faster, faster than I was able to fly. Right when my feet touched the ground his hand brushed my hair and held onto my wings so I could not get away from him. "Give me that amulet!" He put his hand around my amulet and ripped it from my neck. When he took the necklace off, my wings disintegrated and fell to blue ash on the ground.

"What is wrong with you?" I say angrily.

He did not say a word; he held the amulet tight in his hand and crushed it to a powder and placed it into a small pouch. When he looked back at me his eyes look a deeper blue. "Remember you mean nothing to me. You can no longer fly which means you can no longer get away and have no one to protect you." He moved close to me and put his hands around my neck. I gasped as his hands got tighter, and he lifted me off the ground. "Esom…. What…. Are…. You…. doing?"

He started to laugh and as I looked into his eyes I could see the red start to struggle to take control. As they changed his grip loosened, when his eyes turned red and tightened when they turned blue. After a few minutes of this I was about to lose consciousness; his eyes were a solid red again and he let go with the look of fear on his face.

Chapter Fifteen

"What is wrong with you?" I gasped while I grabbed my neck, stood up and I took a few steps back.

"Oh no! Don't tell me I hurt you?" He said with the look of fear.

"Yes, you were trying to kill me. You took my amulet and crushed it."

"No! I couldn't have.... No.... I can't lose control." He took a few steps back and stumbled on a rock.

"What are you talking about lose control?"

"Nothing...."

Esom stepped back a few more feet, then quickly took off and flew out of sight. I was extremely confused, I had no idea what just happened. I stumbled my way back to camp while rubbing my neck. Starlin and Grend were both asleep curled up next to each other by the dimming fire. I walked over to them to see if I could wake Starlin. She didn't move in the slightest, I started to have tears run down my cheeks but I was doing my hardest to make sure I was not making a sound for them to hear.

I sat on the opposite side of the fire with my knees to my chest and arms wrapped around my legs moping. "What happened? Why all of a sudden was he was trying to kill me?" I recalled back to Ethorn when he had that same look in his eyes as he was telling me that I meant nothing to him then as well. I did not care that I meant nothing to him for I did not have feelings for him. Why would a guard of the royal family who is supposed to protect me be trying to kill me? Was I in denial about my feelings or did I not really know what they were? I could not remember most of what had happened over the last few weeks, and at that point I was not sure if I really wanted to know.

"Should I keep going? I didn't want to leave Starlin but she was acting different and if I traveled by myself I could get home faster.

"I don't think I am ready to be Queen but I cannot just leave my father to die without him being able to see me for one last time," I very quietly whispered to myself.

I started to cry again, and this time I was not able to keep myself quiet. I did my best to stay quiet but Grend and Starlin started to stir. I stood up and walked a little ways from the fire so that I was still in the light but they no longer are stirring. "Please forgive me, Starlin, I cannot take this anymore." I turned to continue up the mountain. "I think if I make it to the top I can see where my father's castle is and make it back home in time."

It was still a long way to the top but I was determined to make it there. I was tired and wanted to sleep, but I knew that I had to keep moving. I felt like I had walked forever. As I looked back down to where I had left them I could only see the glow of the fire as if it was a star in the night sky. It did not feel as though I had traveled as far as I did in such a short amount of time. I sighed as I looked up to the top of the mountain. I still had a long way to go, but I desperately needed to make it to the top.

Chapter Sixteen

I took a few more steps up, when I stumbled on a rock and face planted in the dirt. The ground was shaking while it was caving in on its self under my feet. I dropped down a hole. I reached for anything that could keep me from falling, but I was not able to grab onto anything. I screamed for help, my voice does not echo.

I looked down to see if I could see the end. I started to see a small light as it gets bigger and brighter. I heard water dripping below me. It sounded like there was a cave at the end as the drop echoed. I fell through the opening and landed in a pool of water. When I surfaced I gasped for air and swam to the closest edge I could see. I pulled myself up and lay on what felt like grass. I closed my eyes for what felt like a few minutes.

As I opened my eyes and looked around, the cave was bigger than I thought. The ceiling had crystals sticking out of it in every direction possible, even over-lapping one another. They had a blue glow just like the rest of the forest. When I looked down to what I thought was grass, it was actually fur and lots of it.

The ground was lined with all different types of furs. I looked around in fear that I had fallen into the den of a very large creature. I did not see any creatures, but I did see a door which made me a little relaxed for I did not have to worry about a large creature anymore. Even though I did not have to worry about something large, what or who could be the one collecting all this fur and laying it out like this by the water?

I looked up at the hole, thinking I might be able to crawl back out, but the hole was gone as if something was luring me here. I get up and walked towards the door, as I turned the knob it was locked. I heard a set of keys on the other side and quickly got behind the door as the handle moved and the door slowly opened.

I saw the shadow of who I believed was the owner of the cave. It was feline, long and tall. It walked on the balls of its feet, and was carrying a spear. Its tail twitched as its head looked around the room. There was only one creature who had this type of body; it was the Congs. They were peaceful creatures, not that many were left after the great war of ages passed. Not that much is known about them either. After the war no one knew what had happened to them, it was as though they just up and vanished.

Even though legend had said they vanished for someone reason or another, somehow, I ended up finding their den. How lucky of me, I did not know if they were safe to be around or if I should get out of here as soon as possible. The Cong stood in the door-way for quite a while. I could see it move its head as if searching for something. Once it closed the door, the Cong locked the door again and I was stuck in the room with no way out. I did not want to chance me running into one and not knowing what could happen. I had to find a way out of here and fast.

I walked over to the door to see if there was by any chance that it wasn't really locked or if I was able to get the door off its hinges. As I wiggled the handle it was definitely locked, no way was I going to be able to get the door opened that way. I looked for hinges, it was my luck that there was none. I was trapped with no way out.
"No. How am I going to be able to get out now?"

I saw a shadow under the door stop in front of the door as if it heard me speak. I put my hand over my mouth thinking that was going to help me. Just as my luck would have it I sneezed right as the shadow was walking away. It quickly stopped moved back in front of the door and I then heard keys. My heart was pounding I needed somewhere to hide quickly. I looked around and I saw my only chance of hiding was in the pool. I ran over and quickly but quietly lowered myself into the pool just as the door was opening. It seemed as soon as I got my head under water a hand grabbed my wrist and pulled me out.

As I opened my eyes and took a breath I found myself staring into the eyes of a Cong. Cat like eyes, fur silky and beautiful patterns. Her grip was really tight as she hissed. I didn't know what to think or how to act; I was frozen. The Cong, which I noticed was a female tilted her head and stared at me, and when she started to sniff the air around me I sneezed.

She dropped me back in the water then quickly reached for me again and picked me up. I was thrown over her shoulder and she carried me out of the room which she locked on her way out. I was squirming trying to get out of her grip, but she was strong. It's as though she did not mind me squirming, she continued to walk as if she wasn't carrying me over her shoulders. She carried me down the hall and into a cell. When she put me down I heard Starlin.

"Kia, what are you doing here?" she called as she rushed to me.

"What are you doing here? Where is Grend?"

"Grend they dragged away somewhere, I have no idea where. Where is Esom?"

I looked down towards the ground avoiding the question. "How did they get you?" I said, as I looked at her.

"I just woke up to someone grabbing me and Grend, they blindfolded us and when it was taken off I was here and they were dragging him off down the hall."

A female Cong walked over to the cell. "Be quiet, no one told you to speak." Her voice was unsettling and cruel. She walked off, once she was out of sight I rushed over to the cell door to see if could find a way to open it. As I looked I cut my hand on piece of metal on the hinge. My necklace that was given to me by my mother started to glow blue and so did the cut on my hand. Once the glow was gone my hand was no longer cut and felt better than it ever did before.

As I stared at my hand, my necklace and the cell door started to glow white. I heard the lock on the door click and the cell door slowly creaked open. Starlin quickly got up grabbed my hand and pulled me out of the cell. Once we were out, the door closed and locked itself. My necklace and the door stopped glowing. "What just happened?"

"No idea but I am going to go find Grend. C'mon, Kia, lets go find him."

Chapter Seventeen

Quietly we walked down the hallway. We could hear voices, laughter and music off in the distance that echoed down the hall. There were no doors in the hallway besides the door that I can only assume was the one that I was carried through. We followed the echoing sounds when we saw movement in a room just ahead of us. Starlin and I moved closer, the closer we got the more Starlin was pushing me in front of her. I heard only one male laughing, as the rest sounded female. A guard walked past the door, as if heading to join the laughter. We stopped hoping she wouldn't see us.

She did not stop, I sighed in relief as Starlin pushed me closer to the room. I looked into the room and saw a bunch of females surrounding a male sitting in a chair like a King. I looked closer and saw that it was Grend talking and laughing with the females. Starlin snuck up close behind me, looked into the room and yelled. "Grend!" She was mad as she ran over to him.

The guards closest to Starlin grabbed their spears and pointed them towards us. Grend stood. "No. Don't they are my friends." The guards put down their weapons as Grend approached Starlin. As soon as he reached her he passionately kissed her. Starlin goes went in the knees and held him tighter. "I am so confused, what is going on?" Frustrated, I placed my hands on my aching head. Once they stop kissing I was expecting Starlin to pass out, instead both their eyes were blue and glazed over.

"Put her back in the cell," Grend said as four guards moved towards me.

"Make sure she doesn't escape this time," Starlin snapped, while turning back around to kiss Grend.

"Wait what is going on? Starlin, Grend?

What is going on?"

I was grabbed by the arms by two guards as two other guards poke me with their spears. "Ouch! Starlin, Grend help!" Begging ignored, I was taken back to the cell.

I sat in the cold cell. Why was I put back here and how can I get out? All I want to do is get back to my father. Why does everything keep me from getting back to him? I have no sense of time for there is no light that shines from outside. Tired, I stood up and walked over to the cell door. Taking my mother's pendant I placed it on the metal bars thinking that it was going to glow again and let me out. Tears ran down my face as I pounded the pendant onto the bars. "Work, please work." I fell to my knees and cried harder. "What is going on? There has to be a way out of here."

Behind me a rock in the wall moves, I saw cat-like hands pushing in a blanket and a pillow. I rushed over to the rock right as it was being put back into place. I pulled and scratch but it didn't move. I lay down in the blanket and rested my head on the pillow. Giving up and resting I slowly closed my eyes. "I need rest." My eyes were getting heavy.

Just when I thought I was going to be able to get some sleep I saw a cloud of white smoke start to fill the cell. The cloud was making me dizzy and more tired. I started to hear screaming in the distance.

I have no idea how long I had been out but I heard metal bending and hitting the floor. Am I moving? I felt as though I was being wrapped tighter in the blanket that I was given. I opened my eyes to see if I could see what was touching me. Everything around me was blurry, I was only able to make out a faint outline of shadows around me. I was being dragged on the cold floor, still I had no sense of my surroundings. It felt as if the ground became softer. I opened my eyes again hoping this would change my vision. I still could only faintly see the figure that was dragging me. The figure was tall, long tail, thick body with horns on top of its head.

I heard the sound of water, as everything started to shake. My heart began to beat faster and my breath was getting heavier. My eyes rolled into the back of my head, as I heard rocks from the ceiling fall to the ground and drop in the water. I was picked up by what looks like the creature's mouth. What looks like wings, opened and took off through the hole that had been made in the rock above us as I pass out again.

Chapter Eighteen

I feel hot, my wrists and ankles were hurting. I was tied with what felt like thorns. I slowly opened my eyes to see a bright red glow coming from the fireplace directly in front of me. I moved my arms towards the warmth, I didn't move them too far when I saw they were tied to my feet and then to a chain attached to the wall. In the distance, there was a shadow almost like the one I saw when I was in the cell of the Cong's.

The shadow got bigger and bigger as it moved towards me. A female like I had never seen before walked towards me with a plate of food in a wooden bowl. Her skin looked like a Scale head to toe, but only with the body of a Skin. I had heard rumors of Skins and Scales having offspring that looked like this. Even though it is said that when they are born they are to be killed.

She walked over to a table and placed the food on it. She picked up the chain and tugged it as to let me know that I was to go over to the table. I didn't move, instead I scooted back towards to the wall. This made her mad. She picked up the chain and pulled me towards her. I screamed from the pain of the thorns digging into me. She picked me up by the chain and held me off the ground. As I went to scream again she covered my mouth "Shhhh, don't make a sound."

I turned my head to move her hand. Clenching my jaw, trying not to scream. "Then put me down."

She lowered me down to the floor, and loosened the thorns by speaking to it. The thorns around my wrist loosened just enough for my hands to be free. I stood up while rubbing my wrist and wiping the blood away. "You need to eat." She pushed the plate towards me. "Now eat." She stepped back away from the table and folded her arms.

Her tail is twitching behind her impatiently.

"What if I don't eat?"

"Then I will force you."

I did not like the sound of that, but the food did look really good and I had no idea how long it had been since I had any food. It felt like forever since I last ate. I picked up the bread, smelled it before I took a bite. It smelled so good and tasted like cherry berries. I pick up the funny looking soup and start to drink it. Even though the soup smelled good it did not taste that way at all. After a few swallows I dropped the wooden bowl as it broke on the floor. My stomach turned, I felt my body getting warmer and warmer, and I lost my balance and fall. I looked at her as black foam frothed from my mouth.

"Sorry, I had no choice," she said as she bent down to me. "My name is Somber."

When I awoke, I felt my body warm inside and sick. I did not know what it was that I drank but the taste lingered in my mouth. It was not pleasant. I searched for something to drink to get the taste out of my mouth. I saw a glass of what looked like water on the table. I picked up the glass without thinking, when I went to drink it I stopped. Remembering what had happened when I drank the soup I stop, put the glass down and back away from the table.

I fall to my knees, while coughing up white foam. I start to go into spasms and shaking on the floor. My body temperature was falling, I was getting colder. Just when I thought I was getting colder my temperature started to get hotter. I was sweating, my eyes rolled into the back of my head and I felt like I stopped breathing as I passed out crawling to the fire-place.

When I awoke, the fire had died down, all what was left was embers. I was still tied up but this time it was only one leg and the chain was longer. I followed the chain, it came to a hole in the wall and continued to the other side. I tugged on the chain and it got longer. I got about five feet pulled through the hole when I heard a female voice screaming in pain.

The chain started to move out of my hand and back through the hole. I quickly grabbed the chain and it continued to pull through the wall hurting my hands. Within a few seconds the whole chain was through the wall and my leg was being pulled up against the hole.

I screamed in pain. The female was speaking but I could not understand her. Her voice was muffled and distorted, the chains loosened and where the light was coming in from the hole now got dark.

"Just sit still and you will not get hurt."

"What is going on? I feel really warm and sick at the same time."

"I cannot tell you."

"Why are you chained up to me?"

"I am now supposed to be your keeper. We are both prisoners here."

"Keeper? If you're my keeper why are you on the other side of this wall?"

"It is the way of the master."

"What master?"

"He is the one who took you from the Congs' prison cell."

"Where are we?"

"You sure do ask a lot of questions. I know more about you than you think. I am only allowed to give you so much information. I can talk to you but I am not supposed to."

"If you know so much about me, and I know nothing about you, can you give me your name?"

"My name is Somber, I told you that already when I brought you your food."

"Wait, you are the one who made me sick?"

"Yes."

"What did you do to me? I feel warm and sick."

"It will pass. The effects are only temporary. It is a way for him to track you."

"Track me? Who would want to track me?"

"I cannot tell you yet."

"Why are you…"

"I did say you ask a lot of questions. I can no longer answer any more questions. If you speak to me I will not answer you."

"Wait, what?"

The ground shook but it did not feel like a quake. It felt like a Scale walking, a very large Scale. I wondered if that is who took me? I could not be for sure that was who it was. Why did a Scale want me? There is more to this story than what I know. I have to find a way out of here but first I need to get this chain off me and get rid of this 'Somber' girl I am tied up with.

Looking around the room there was only a table, bed, chair, and a fire-place. I did not see a door. How could I get into a room without a door? The fireplace vent was too small to fit someone through. I felt around my neck wanting to hold onto my mother's necklace. I needed her comfort right now. When I felt my neck the necklace was gone. "Where is it?"

I franticly searched the room and patted myself down thinking that it fell off or was somewhere in the room.

"Now, where is it?"

It was gone, nowhere in the room or on me. I had lost my necklace! I sat down and started to cry.

"Be quiet, he will hear you."

"I don't care."

All I could think about was my mother and how it was the last thing she gave me. A tiny hole in the wall opened and a plate of food came into the room. I wanted to eat but remembering what happened last time I ate the food that was given to me I was hesitant.

"You better eat."

"Why? So the same thing can happen to me like it did last time I ate anything that was given to me?"

"No, that was the only time."

I pondered whether what Somber said was true or not. I crawled over to the food, the smell was really good and I still was not sure if I wanted to eat it. Even though the first time I ate, the smell was really good the soup was horrible. There was no soup this time, maybe it would be safe to eat. I picked up the cherry berries one at a time and eat them. So far so good, the funny taste was not there. I geo through eating all the food but the last dew weed. I picked it up wanting to eat it but something was telling me not to. I ignored my thoughts and popped it into my mouth.

Chapter Nineteen

I felt warm again, this time the feeling was a little better. My head started to get fuzzy, I didn't mind the feeling though. I made my way over to the fire, sat and stared into the embers. I saw fire bugs that looked like Skins dancing around and around. They seemed happy and care-free, but something was wrong. One of the fire bugs was crying over in the corner of the embers while the others played.

I continued watching and no matter what the little fire bug did, none of the others wanted to play. As I watched the fire bugs seemed to grow in age. They all looked older and the fire bug that was in the corner grew like the rest but she looked completely different than the others. Only its features were more prominent and it was taller than the others.

Watching them ignore the other fire bug was sad. I felt sorry for the little creature. I saw another age jump, they all were older looking, like adult fire bugs. The one that was ignored was still being ignored. This time something was different, instead of keeping its distance from the others. It walked over to the others and started attacking them.

It went on for quite a while until the other fire bugs submitted to the larger one. Once they all calmed down and they looked like they were getting along with each other, the larger one pointed to one of the other fire bugs, while the others jumped on the fire bug and killed it.

When it then turned and pointed towards me, the other fire bugs jumped out of the embers and walked towards me. Burning the ground as they walked, I was mesmerized and didn't move. As they move closer and closer I get warmer and warmer. One touched my foot and I can feel it burn, I didn't move or make a sound. It was as though I was in a trance as they crawled up my legs.

I felt a tug on my leg from the chain, it didn't bother me. The tugging got stronger and stronger as it started to pull me towards the tiny hole in the wall.

"Wake up."

I ignored Somber talking to me. My ankle was bleeding from the thorns digging into me. The fire bugs continued to climb, burning and I still could not feel the pain. There was a sound of running water in the room as I got drenched. This woke me from my daze, the fire bugs sizzled in the water and then vanished.

"What did you do that for?"

"The fire bugs were trying to kill you?"

"What fire bugs?"

"The ones I just extinguished. Get up we need to get out of here."

"Wait. How did you get in here?"

"There is a door, I just chose not to be in the same room as you."

"What door? Why do you want to help me? Are you not my keeper and are you not supposed to keep an eye on me to make sure I do not leave this place for some reason?"

"Yes, I am, but I am also a prisoner as well. I am forced to do the bidding of Mylor."

"Who is that?"

"He is the Scale who keeps me here. I am his prisoner but I also am here of my own free will."

Somber walked over to the fire and added wood from the wood pile to it. The wood was damp and smoked just a little. The chain that was tying us together looked shorter than it did before.

"As you know my kind is never allowed to

live. My mother did not agree with the law and kept me alive till I was able to fend for myself. My father was killed protecting my mother from the mob trying to kill me for being born. I ran away then, if I remember correct I was 10. I don't know what has become of my mother. I know I will never see her again. I was weak and on the verge of dying when Mylor found me, he didn't agree with the law either. He took me in, helped raise me little by little and to understand what I am and what I am capable of. Years after, I started to look up to him like a brother. Then one day he went out, when he came back he was different I didn't know how but he has changed. Ever since I have become a prisoner here. He will not let me leave or do what I want. He keeps me locked up to protect his 'things'."

"I am sorry that you lost your father. Maybe you will see your mother again someday? What do you mean by things?"

"Maybe, but I am not counting on it. I gave up looking for her."

"Why?"

"That is none of your concern."

I stood up rubbing my burns, walked over to the table and picked up the water that was still on the table. I got a drink and placed the cup down, Somber was right next to me staring at me deeply wide eyed.

"What? Why are you looking at me like that?"

She got really close to me, placed one of her hands on my chin as to hold me still so she can examine me closely. She gets closer and closer almost touching nose to nose. She is staring deeply into my eyes.

"Why does he want you so bad?"

Her eyes widened, she let go of me and stepped back.

"That is why?"

"What are you talking about?"

"You are the princess, Kia. You're the heir to the throne."

"Yes, how did you know that?"

"I have many powers. I am able to look into your eyes and see all of your past. You have companions. Grend, Esom who are both halflings. Ones who do not look like me, they are like you. You have a female companion Starlin. You care deeply for her and would do anything for her."

"You can tell all of that? Then you must know why I must leave?"

"I do. I saw that you are in pain. Your father the King is dying. If the legends are true you need to get back to him before he passes on."

Somber stopped talking, right when I was about to ask her a question. "Quiet." There were loud noises coming from somewhere in the chamber. Somber, without a word walked over to the wall where the hole was, placed her hand on the wall as a door opened up. The chain that was tying us together was getting long again. She went through the door and it closed behind her leaving only a hole for the chain.

The sound got louder and louder, then the floor started to rumble. The rumbling was not like an earthquake. It was a Skin walking. The sound of each foot step sounded like the whole room was going to fall apart. As embers jumped out of the fire place I get my footing and grabbed on to the stone table.

I had no idea what was going on. Never have I felt the footsteps of a Skin this bad before. I was getting terrified, not knowing what to expect. As the footsteps got closer I continued to try and keep my balance. Finally, it stopped, right on the other side of my wall. My racing heart was heavy with fear. As the wall began to vanish I started to breathe heavy, the room went cold and I can see my breath.

I waited for what I was about to see, frightened what I might see on the other side. The wall started to disappear but looked only transparent, I was able to see the hallway where the Scale was waiting.

I was right, he was one of the largest Scales I had ever seen. He looked as though he was too big for the hallway. His piercing green eyes stared right at me, and he was growling. He was white, horns bigger than my father's. Spikes all the way down his back, to his pointed tail that looked like a sword. His breath was like snow as it formed on the transparent wall as ice crystals appeared. He slammed his tail on the floor and I stumbled with the vibrations.

The room got colder and his breath got heavier. I watched the floor as it turned to ice and everything around the room started to freeze, even the small flames froze in place. The ice slowly moved up my legs. "What is going on?" I was franticly saying trying to move my legs. There was no answer from him, just more heavy breathing.

The more I struggled to move the faster the ice moved up my body. Soon the ice was covering everywhere and making its way up my neck. I feared the worst, for that he was trying to kill me. Not only were the Shades wanting me dead, now he does as well. This cannot be the end for I still need to make my way back to my father. I am now completely covered in ice, I feel that I am dead for I cannot hold my breath that long.

I struggled to hold my breath. As I exhaled and expected the worst, to my surprise the ice was not touching my face and I was able to breathe freely. I could not move and was starting to panic. Mylor took a deep breath and let it out covering the transparent wall turning it fully to ice. With a slam of his massive tail the ice wall broke apart and he stepped into the room. The room was smaller than the hallway for he could hardly fit.

"The Dark Master will have you. I will take you alive, let the Dark Master have the thrill of killing you."

I couldn't believe what I was hearing. Mylor was working for the Dark Master? I wished I hadn't left Starlin and Grend, they would be able to help me get out of this. Or I might not even be in this mess in the first place. I was hoping that Esom was going to sweep into the room and save me but then I remembered what happened before I ended up here. He was trying to kill me.

I was confused and I didn't know what to do or how to react. Mylor took the tip of his tail and touched the wall in which Somber was behind. As the wall vanished Somber knew exactly what Mylor wanted her to do, for all she did was nod and grab the cart that she was sitting next to.

"Somber, why are you doing this?"

My question was left un-answered. She was not able to hear me through the thick ice. With her strength, she lifted me up and placed me on the cart with ease. Mylor backed out of the room with Somber following pulling me behind her with the chain.

Chapter Twenty

Once out of the room the wall became solid rock again. With each step Mylor took the floor where his foot was touching would turn to ice, once he lifted his foot the ice would quickly melt. I was astonished by what I saw, I did not know there was a Scale that could control the snow. The hallway was slowly getting bigger for Mylor's spikes were no longer getting pushed down and he started to stand up.

Bigger and bigger the hallway got until it came to a giant open room lit with blue light and gold everywhere. The floor was blue marble with gold flakes intertwined with green emeralds. His throne in the center was made out of red and black marble. As Mylor fully stood up, I was able to see how big he really was. He stood almost 25 feet tall, my father only stood 16. I thought my father was big for being a Scale, it looks as though I was wrong.

In the hall, I did not see his wings but in this great room I could. He opened his wings and stretched them from being cramped in the hallway. With the shimmer of light hitting his wings they looked as though they were transparent. Once he was done he sat down on a pile of snow and wrapped his tail around the cart I was on, pulling me towards him.

"Why does the Dark Master want you so badly? You might be the princess, but what is so special about you?"

"Somber, send a message to the Dark Master saying we have the princess and will have her there shortly."

Somber nodded and walked out of the room. She was still attached to me with the chain which grew longer and longer as she walked off. Mylor got closer to me looking through the ice wanting a better glimpse of me. His massive claw tapped on the ice. "You could be a toy. Maybe I should keep you as a pet…. or I could just eat you?"

I was getting nervous not wanting to be this Skin's next meal. Mylor turned me around and around as if toying with me. I was getting sick, trying not to vomit. Mylor stopped spinning me around as he wrapped his tail around me and squeezed till the ice started to crack.

Mylor continued tapping on the ice as though he was taunting that he had me captured. "I will get rewarded for this." My body was getting colder by the second. Starting to shiver, I wanted out and to be warm. I thought of fire, hopefully that will help keep warm. I could feel my body getting warm from the inside as if it was helping.

I didn't want to lose the feeling of being warm so I kept my eyes closed. A sudden jerking of the cart made me snap out of my self-induced trance. My temperature was dropping again once I opened my eyes. Somber was standing next to me. She looked different somehow then she did before. Her eyes were glazed over, breathing heavy while pacing back and forth staring at me.

Water was dripping on my face. Mylor growls at Somber who was ignoring him and continues to pace back and forth. "Somber." With a hard thud of his tail Somber snapped out of it.

"Sorry, Mylor. I did not mean to cause alarm," I said, bowing towards him.

"Somber, when did you last eat?"

"This morning." She bent down to one knee as to apologize for her actions.

"This morning? It seems that the shadowing

spell is warring off quicker by the day. Go eat, now! I cannot afford to lose you."

"Yes, Mylor." Getting up she walked off.

"Now to mend what she tried to undo." Mylor took a big breath and slowly breathed on me hardening the ice.

I was not getting out of this anytime soon. I closed my eyes again hoping that I could get warm by thinking of the fire again and adding images of the warm sunshine. I imagined being on a beach in my swimsuit laying on the hot sand and drinking in the warm sun. Then dark clouds covered the sun blocking the sunlight as a cold breeze blew and the water started to freeze. I got extremely cold, this was not working,

I began to imagine that I was sitting next to a warm raging fire wrapped in several large blankets drinking a cup of nice hot white angel flower tea. I started to feel warm, then the fire went out and the tea froze solid. The room became extremely cold. I opened my eyes disappointed, thinking of fire was not helping me this time.

Somber walked back into the room. "I have sent a message to the Dark Master. The Dark Master replied awaiting for Kia's arrival."

Mylor grinned deeply, showing his massive teeth. "Somber, go be a good girl and fetch me something for a snack. I am starving with excitement."

"Yes, Mylor." She left the room but this time through a different door. She was only gone for what seemed like seconds when she came back in carrying a giant boar in with her.

I was shocked for the boar was still alive, screaming and fighting to get out of Somber's grip. She placed the boar down in front of Mylor as it tried to run off Mylor quickly placed a claw on the boar's tail. Screeching and digging into the icy floor was of no use. Mylor pulled the boar back towards him and with two claws picked it up by the tail and placed the animal in his mouth.

He closed his mouth but did not chew. He let's the boar squirm in his mouth for what seemed like forever before he swallowed the boar whole. I was mortified, how can he treat animals this way? I felt bad the way it had died like that.

"Somber, shall we get going? I don't want to keep our Dark Master waiting?"

Somber picked up the chain and pulled me toward her. My gut sank, I wanted to be back home with my dad. Not trapped in ice on my way to the Dark Master. I started to wish I never left back when I was young. I knew I was going to die, that is all the Dark Master does, is kill and kill. No remorse at all.

Somber continued to pull me with the chain out of the room with Mylor following close behind swinging his tail back and forth throwing ice spikes everywhere. Some seemed to vanish as they hit the walls and floor. Once his tail was completely out of the throne room he slammed it on the floor and caused the entrance to his throne room to freeze over.

Somber continued down the hallway. The walls were more jagged, cob webs were everywhere. I saw paintings on the wall but I could not make out what they were for the paintings has frost all over them.

The floor was no longer like the one in Mylor's throne room. It was black and grey. I was pulled past doors that were torn apart and put back together. As well as ones with bars for windows. Some had dents in the wooden doors. It was as though I was not the only one ever to be captured by Mylor.

Somber placed one of her hands on the wall and dragged it past one door. The door was clean, unaltered, and the bars were made of crystals. It was odd that this one door out of all the others were like this. It made me wonder what was on the other side of it. With her gesture I thought that maybe this was Somber's room. She stopped when her hand reached the doorknob, looking back without a word she stares at Mylor. He did not say anything, just huffed while snow came out his nose. She let go of the knob as a tear ran down her cheek. This room must have more meaning to her than it appears.

Somber scowled at Mylor and continued down the hallway. It opened up into a larger room that was big but not quite as big the throne room. This room was the opposite of Mylor's throne room, there was nothing shining. Everything was lifeless and dull. The only things I could make out were the wood piles in the corner, a larger cart that Somber was walking over to. A fireplace that looked only like embers.

There was a table in the center of the room with wooden bowls and plates. This looked like the kitchen. "Now, Somber. Finish gathering your supplies to make the Shadowing Spell so our way out you will not lose control."

"Yes, Mylor," she said as she bowed her head.

At the cupboard, she began pulling out several bowls and a wooden pot. She opened another cupboard and grabs Cherry Berries, Dew weed, bread, and a vial of something black. I was not sure what it could be but my gut said it was the Shadowing Spell.

She placed everything in a leather bag, which looked like it would not all fit. Everything did fit, as she threw it over her should it laid flat as if there was nothing in it. Still only with the chain she continued to pull me.

Mylor slammed his tail again as another

wall opened and I could see outside. It was sunny, the grass was really green. I was no longer in the Sapphire Woods. I had no idea where I was, I was far away from my friends and possibly further from my father. With me being taken to the Dark Master maybe I will be even further from him.

Chapter Twenty-One

After Mylor stepped out of the cave and slammed his tail again on the ground, the cave wall re-appeared again, blending perfectly into the rest of the wall making it look as though there was no opening. I was astonished at what power Mylor had, I had never seen one so powerful before.

With the sun beating down on us, Mylor shimmered which you could tell he did not like that much. With the swish of his tail he formed a cloud of snow above him to keep him cold. In order to keep the ice from melting, Mylor made sure to keep me close to him and slowly blow onto me keeping the ice solid.

The ground out here was a lot bumpier than it was in the cave. I was hoping that one of these bumps was going to make me tip over and break the ice, then I would be free from him and maybe have a chance to escape. We were not more than about one mile from the cave when Somber stopped and fell to her knees.

"Somber, what's wrong?"

"I need to make the Shadowing Spell again. It's weakening quicker and quicker. I do not know if we have enough supplies to make it to the Dark Master, Mylor. Shall I make the Shadowing Spell, then go find more Shade Sap to last till we get to the Dark Master?"

"Yes. Be quick about it. You know I hate being in the sun."

"Yes, Mylor."

She snapped her fingers as a hole was formed in the ground. Somber walked off behind the trees but was not gone long. She came back bringing a small pile of sticks and kindling. Neatly she arranged the pile in the hole, with another snap of her fingers the pile started to burn.

She reached into her bag and pulled out the wooden pot, spoon, bowl, a jar of water, dew weed and the small vial of Shade Sap. "Use the whole vial, I do not want you to lose control again." Somber nodded and dumped the whole vial into the pot. She poured half of the jar of water into the pot while mixing. She grabbed the dew weed and tossed the whole thing into the pot. Placing the wooden pot over the fire it did not burn like I thought it would.

She stirred some more then put the spoon to her mouth. With a bitter look on her face and a sense of calming she took a deep breath and exhaled smoke. After shaking her head, she reached into the bag, grabbed the cherry berries, and tossed them into the pot while smashing them with the spoon. After sitting there till the sun's rays had moved behind the trees she poured the thick soup into a bowl.

Somber whispered to the soup before she quickly drank the Shadowing Spell. Once the bowl was empty she dropped it into the fire. Her eyes widened and her back arched. Black foam started to come out of her mouth, and she fell backwards onto the forest floor. Her body started to convulse and her tail swung around wildly.

Somber stopped moving and looked as though she had stopped breathing. I stared horrified that it had killed her. Then her tail twitched, as she slowly moved her arm to help her sit up. Somber's eyes were black, as she blinked her eyes slowly changed back to their previous blue color. She wiped the remaining foam from her mouth and stood up. She blew on the fire which put it out.

"Feel better?"

"Yes, Mylor. I hope this lasts long enough till I can find more Shade Sap."

She gathered up all the supplies besides the pot she used and put them back into her bag. She walked over to a tree and dumped the pot onto the roots. I watched as the tree slowly turned black, withered and crumbled to ash. I wondered why she didn't keep the soup and use it later.

Somber walked over to me and this time she grabbed the cart instead of the chain. Her feet were dragging on the ground, her body seemed more lethargic than it did before. Mylor started to laugh and Somber turned around.

"What it is?"

"I just thought, what if something were to happen to the little princess," he said as he tapped the ice with his claw. "An accident that could kill her. Then I would be able to eat her," he said, laughing harder. "Oh wait, I know what my reward could be for bringing you back to the Dark Master. The Dark Master can let me eat you. That would be a great reward and we both could get what we want."

Mylor's way of thinking was making me nervous. I didn't want to be his next meal. I had to get out of here but I really did not know how I was going to do that. Maybe if I rocked myself back and forth I could tip over and break the ice. That sounded like a great idea but then I got to thinking that would be a bad idea. I don't think I would be able to move all too well after being a popsicle for this long. It was about mid-day when we stopped abruptly.

"Mylor, do you think she needs to warm up a little bit so she does not freeze to death before we get there?"

"That is a good point. We want our Dark Master to be the one to kill her."

Somber stepped close to me, she placed one hand on the ice and the other on her chest. Taking a deep breath and exhaling, steam started to come out of the nose. Her hand that was touching the ice glowed red, her hand on her chest started to shake as the steam poured out of her nose faster and faster.

The steam started to swirl around me. Somber's

hand on the ice was now moving in a circular motion causing the ice to melt. The steam circling me was becoming thicker. Under Somber's hand a hole started to form. The steam moved from around the ice and into the hole.

The cold sensation was no longer there as the ice started to melt from the inside. The dripping water was sending chills up my spine. The ice started to thin very rapidly, and I began to see sun shining through the top of the ice. I was able to feel the sun's rays, it was warm and inviting.

I thought I was going to collapse on the ground and just lay in the sun soaking up the rays but I was still not able to move. Even though my head and upper body were no longer frozen my legs still were. I could feel the cold sensation of the ice around my legs and the warm sensation of the heat on my upper body.

I started to shiver, wrapping my arms around me to rub my body to induce circulation. Somber took one step towards me and touched my arm. With a quick deep breath and an exhale my body was dry. Somber handed me some bread. "Eat."

I grabbed the bread from her and started to eat it slowly. If I took my time eating it would be that much longer before I had to get covered in the ice again. The bread was only a small piece and was gone in two small bites. Somber handed me small handful of cherry berries. I started to eat them one at a time, savoring the sun's warmth for as long as I possibly could.

Mylor's tail started to twitch. "Hurry," he demanded as he flapped his wings. I put the last two cherry berries in my mouth. Mylor started to breathe again on me, the ice started to crawl up my legs.

"Wait!" I said quickly. "Can I at least have some

water to wash down the food?"

Mylor didn't stop breathing, he only slowed down how fast the ice was crawling. Somber filled a cup with water and handed it to me. I drank it, and handed her back the cup. Once Somber's hands were clear, Mylor took a deep breath and let it out. In a second I was covered back in ice. In an instant I felt the cold again, doing my best to hold onto the warmth for as long as I could. The warmth started to fade as I could feel the cold creep into my bones. I hated how cold I was and just wanted back in the sunlight.

"Now get moving."

"Yes, Mylor."

Somber quietly pulled me again, this time with a quicker pace than before. It was the peak of heat with the sun blazing down on us. Somber was sweating pulling me, even though I was shivering from the cold I was wishing I was in the heat sweating in the sun with Somber. I couldn't keep my eyes open as the cold was getting to me.

Chapter Twenty-Two

I closed my eyes for what felt like a second hoping that it would make time go faster just so I could get out of this ice prison. I opened my eyes to see fairies swarming around Mylor with his blizzard and Somber's fire blaze. The fairies that got too close to them were dying.

I could see Esom swooping down, landing next to Somber. "Esom.... Help me!" My screams were not to be heard. Esom flew into the air then quickly headed towards the ground while landing with a thud knocking Somber over. Mylor flicked his tail towards Esom and hit him dead in the back.

He fell to the ground while I was screaming, "Esom, get up!" He was not moving, the ground around him was being stained red. Black Angel Flower vines appeared and started to cover his body. As I cried, my tears froze to my cheeks and it stung. Somber walked over to Esom while throwing fireballs.

I watched horrified as she got closer and closer to him. Then the black angel flowers glowed white, and extinguished her fireballs. My tears turned red, melted and ran down my face. The red tears dripped on the ice as a hole appeared and the red tears floated in front of me in a swirling pattern as it slowly moved towards Esom.

I couldn't comprehend what was going on. The red start to blend with the white turning pink. I felt my heart skip a beat as I gasped for air. I could hear Esom's voice even though he was not moving. "Listen, I am sorry for what I did. I was not myself. I cannot tell you why, but in time you will see. I am sorry for my actions and I hope that you can forgive me. Goodbye."

The pink grew larger and larger and the ice was

melting. I closed my eyes again not sure what was going on. I opened my eyes and to my surprise it was all a dream. I didn't think I was asleep that long. As a matter of fact, I know it was not, for we had not moved that far. Was I starting to hallucinate, was the cold affecting me that much?

My stomach was growling and aching, hunger was hitting me hard, and I don't think they would stop again till we got to the Dark Master. It was almost dusk, the sky was turning purple and green, colors I had never seen before. Something was in the air and it was chilling my bones even more than the ice itself.

Chapter Twenty-Three

The nighttime air was making it even colder for me. I started to shiver which was making it harder for me to breathe. I was not able to keep my eyes open for much longer. I didn't want to fall asleep. I was afraid of more nightmares, but even still fighting sleep, I fell asleep anyways.

I woke up suddenly to water dripping on my face. The ground was shaking, I could make out flashes of red light mixed with flashes of white light. I could feel that I was being pulled in many directions but I couldn't tell why.

The white and red flashes got larger and brighter, the thinner the ice melted. As the ice completely melted I fell out of the cart and onto the ground. Shivering as I curled into a ball while starting to fall asleep, I felt someone pick me up.

"Kia. Wake up, it's not time to lay down, we need to get you out of here."

"Starlin…. How did you find me?" I said, my teeth chattering.

"Not now, I will tell you shortly."

Fire fly's pass me and hits Mylor. I could finally see what was going on around me. Somber and Grend were fighting Mylor. I could see no sign of Esom and it had me really worried for what I saw in my dream. Starlin stood me up the rest of the way. "Now let's go." We made our way to the edge of the wood line and out of the view of the fight going on behind us.

Grend and Somber hit Mylor as hard as they could with all their strength. Somber's fire was making Mylor weak and he was not able to fight back. Grend was using his sword that was enchanted by Somber's flame.

Grend swung his sword towards Mylor as it grazed his leg. "Why you!" Mylor hissed towards Grend. Somber threw fire towards him. Mylor used his ice breath to extinguish the fire. Somber threw another fireball towards him. While Mylor was distracted with the first fireball, the second curved around Mylor's body and landed on his wing.

The fire burned through his wing like an ice cube thrown into a fire pit. As he screamed in pain, Grend quickly chopped the bottom half of his tail off. Mylor screamed again and used his good wing to throw Grend.

Somber moved in close while making a sword out of her fire. As Grend picked up his sword, Mylor swung what little tail he had left towards him. Grend jumped onto Mylor's back, placed his sword above his head and plunged it into Mylor's spine, dropping the beast to the ground.

Somber had been waiting for this chance to finally take Mylor out so she could be free again and no longer in his control. She rushed him, with a quick swing of her flame sword and sliced his neck as his body went limp. The last breath that was in his body seeped out of his neck and formed a cloud of snow above his body while snowing down on him.

"We must get out of here. There is no true way to kill him. This has only stunned him for a short time. This will give us time to escape."

Somber shortened the chain slowly as she followed it. I was huddled in a ball while Starlin was rubbing me to help raise my body temperature. Somber got really close to me as I scooted away from her. With her hands, she formed a shield of fire around me. I could feel the warmth as I finally began to warm up again.

I slowly opened my eyes to see Somber with Grend and Starlin. Once Somber put down her hands the flames vanished. I quickly stood up while taking a few steps back from Somber.

"Get away from me!"

"I am trying to help you."

"No, you work for the Dark Master and was taking me to be killed."

"Let me explain."

"No, I don't want to hear any explanation from you. You were trying to kill me."

"Kia, I wasn't trying to have you killed. I sent for Grend and Starlin to help me rescue you from Mylor. I was trying to protect you. I know what will happen if you don't get back to your father and take your place as Queen."

I started to walk off when my leg got pulled back and I fell on my face. "Let me go," I whined, tugging on the chain.

"I can't take the chain off. The only one who can remove the chain is Mylor."

"You're telling me we're stuck together?"

"Yes, but there is a way to get the chain off of us. You just have to trust me that I can get it off."

Mylor's body started to twitch as his wounds were healing. He opened his eyes and roared so loudly that the ground shook. "Quickly, we need to move. He will be here any second."

"What!"

Somber grabbed my hand and started to run as Starlin and Grend followed right behind. Running as fast as we could was not doing much good. With every step, we took the ground shook making it very hard for us to run. "Quickly, we have to hide. He will kill all of us for what we did!"

I looked behind me and saw that Mylor was close behind. With his massive size, I was able to see him in the distance ripping trees out his way and throwing them aside like a stick.

I abruptly stopped as my toes hung off the edge of a cliff. Somber grabbed my arm and pulled me back. "Careful, Princess, you don't want to fall to your death, do you?"

"What are we going to do now? He's almost here."

"There is a cave just beneath us. Mylor can't fly, if you get down there he won't be able to get to you."

"How are we supposed to get down there? We have no rope." Grend looked over the side of the cliff and saw the cave she was talking about. "That is really a long drop."

"Kia, you will have to go down first. I can lower you using the chain. After you are down Starlin and Grend will follow."

"What will happen to you? Won't he just pull Kia up using this chain?" Starlin asked.

"I can enchant the chain so he can't touch it. Don't worry about me. If he kills me then the chain will break. Don't worry, it will be worth it. I don't deserve to live with all the wrong that I have done in my life, letting him control me and helping him try to kill the future Queen. Now go, before it's too late."

We walked over to the edge. "Don't worry about holding on, just let me lower you down. Tug on the chain once you have reached the cave." I let go of the edge, and let her lower me. With the ground shaking from each of Mylor's steps I bumped on the cliff-side and started to bleed on my shoulders. I reached the cave and swung myself to the opening, and as I tugged on the chain it stopped growing.

Soon I could see the chain move and saw Starlin's feet. I helped her into the cave and Grend soon followed. Once Grend was in the cave he tugged on the chain again. It started to grow again, then it stopped. As quickly as the ground stopped shaking, I heard Somber scream and the chain fell. The shackle that was attached to my leg flickered and started to vanish.

"Quickly, grab the chain!" Grend said as he reached for the chain. "Somber told me that even if the shackles are removed the chain will stay however long it is for a couple of days. That way we can still continue on down the cliff-side."

Mylor roared, "Where is she, Somber? Somber, answer me! I will find you, Princess, the Dark Master will kill you and take the throne from you."

Somber's body was all I saw falling off the cliff-side.

"Somber!"

Chapter Twenty-Four

I ran over to the cave entrance thinking that I was going to be able to catch her, but I couldn't. I watched as she fell landing in the riverbed below. "Hurry, we must get to her. She might still be alive." I grabbed the chain from Grend and threw it out of the cave. I attached the chain to the largest stalagmite I saw. "I hope this holds."

Starlin and Grend followed, almost to the riverbed when the chain started to give. Once my feet touched the ground the chain gave and threw Starlin and Grend on top of me. "Thanks for the catch, Kia."

"Starlin, this is no time to play around. Where is Somber?"

I searched around for her, and I looked down the riverbed. I could see something on the other side of the river caught on a log. "Is that Somber?" I started to walk through the river, I wasn't paying attention to how deep it was and sank into the water. I quickly caught my breath and started to swim to the other side.

"You two coming?"

They didn't say a word, just held hands and started to walk along the riverbed on the other side. I rushed over to what I saw caught on the log. "Somber?" If it was her, she did not look the same as she did before. The part of her that made her look like a Skin was gone, she now looked like a tiny Scale. "Somber? Is that you, Somber? Please, Somber, if that is you say something."

No sound or movement came from the Scale I thought was Somber. I started to cry even though I was not sure why. I hated her, in fact, I was glad she was gone. But still something was wrong, it did not feel right; she should not have died. I reached towards the head of the Scale that lay before me when a white light shined from my hand.

"What is going on?" I looked over at Starlin and Grend to see where they were. I saw them across the river huddled together next to a fire, which was odd for I didn't see them start the fire. In my hand, I felt something appear, it was my mother's necklace. The light shined brighter and brighter until it engulfed the Scale in front of me.

Soon the vial started to crack and then it quickly shattered. My mother in her fairy form was hovering over the top of the Scale smiling. As I watched, a tear rolled down her face as she touched my forehead. "Kia, don't worry about me. One day we will be together again. Let me protect you no longer and give you the friend you need. Let her be the one to protect you now, live your life and be strong for the kingdom and do what is right in your heart. I love you, Kia, very much."

Before I could speak, her light disappeared and all I saw was the Scale in front of me float off the ground, glow white and open her eyes. She was placed on her feet as she stood there staring at me confused.

"What happened?"

"You are Somber, right?"

"Kia? What happened? Last thing I remember was dying."

"Somber." I wrapped my arms around her neck and gave her a hug while crying.

"Can you let go please? You're choking me."

"Sorry." I let her go and stared at her.

"What happened?"

"You died, my mother brought you back to life."

"What? How?"

"She said I needed a friend who was going to protect me."

"What? No one can bring the dead back to life."

"She was a fairy."

"I thought fairies were a myth."

"Yes, they were, but that is a story for another time. Can I ask you a question?"

"Yes, what is it?"

"Why do you look like a baby Scale?"

"Oh." Looking away. "Well when my kind die their body is transformed into the part of them that was more dominant than the other. So, in my case I was more like a Scale than a Skin."

"Will you ever get your Skin side back?"

"I don't know. No one has even been brought back to life. Now let's be done talking about this and get you back to your father."

"Yes, let's go."

I looked over at Grend and Starlin, who acted as though we were not there. I had no idea what was going on between them but I was bound and determined that I was going to find out one way or another. Ever since Ethorn they had been acting very strange, and I did not like it one bit.

"Starlin, Grend, there is a bridge just down the river. We will meet you there, we are really close to my father's kingdom." I yelled across the river towards them, "Let us get going you two!"

They looked over at me and I saw a flash of one eye red and the other was blue in both of them. I started to think that they were not Grend and Starlin but I was not sure and just brushed it off as if it was a hallucination.

"Let's go, Somber."

Chapter Twenty-Five

I looked back over the river wondering if what I saw was just my imagination or not. As I looked forward towards the bridge I was thinking if everything that I was doing was for the right reasons. I wanted to go back and see my father, I did miss him and wanted to be there at the castle but I didn't want things to end up the way they did.

Only if he would have just let me out every once in a while, I bet none of this would have happened. Was I being selfish for acting the way I did? I didn't really want to be Queen, I never had plans on it. I was hoping I would have a sister one day and she could become Queen. Even though my parents adopted Starlin and I did consider her my sister she was never going to be able to take the throne. She was not of royal blood and only royal blood could become Queen.

I started to cry thinking that my mother died before she could have another child. I didn't care what happened to me so long as my friends were safe. Maybe it was time for me to grow up and become the person that my parents had set out for me before I was born.

As we walked towards the bridge, Grend and Starlin were laughing and holding hands. They looked as though they had no care in the world and everything around them was butterflies and rainbows. Somber and I were another story, we both were on edge. Somber kept looking over her shoulder for fear of Mylor coming after her. I was scared that I wasn't going to make it in time to reach my father.

Closer and closer we got to the bridge, I started to wonder what had happened to Esom? Grend had not even brought up the fact that he was not with us anymore, which I thought he would have. They seemed to be inseparable since we met up with them. I wondered if he was ok or if what I saw in my dream was real or not. I couldn't stop thinking about it, I was sacred, I really hoped that it wasn't real, I didn't know what I would do if he ended up dead and it was because of me and what I did to him. The more I thought about it the worse I felt. I wish I could go back to when that happened and make one decision different.

We were at the bridge, it ran above a waterfall. I looked over the edge and to the bottom of the waterfall, and continued to look down into the river below as I followed it out into the distance which led to the coast. I had never seen the coast before, it was really beautiful.

Even though the coast was still a way off in the distance I was able to see the water change color with the setting sun. As I watched, I saw the clouds slowly moving and getting darker around the sun. Soon the sun was hidden as the colors shined through the clouds then disappeared altogether.

"Starlin, Grend, come over to this side, we need to find shelter for the night. We might have a storm coming."

They still did not say a word as they crossed the bridge. My concern for them was growing stronger and stronger. I was anxious wondering how my dad was doing, but also so scared for I knew this was going to be the last time that I was going to see him alive. I didn't know how much more time he had left or if he was even still alive. I didn't want to think about it, but that was all what I could think about.

Starlin and Grend crossed the bridge. Starlin let go of Grend's hand and took a few steps away from him. "Let's go, Kia, I don't want to get caught in this storm either."

"Where do you suggest we go?" Starlin started to walk off away from the bridge, I wasn't sure where she was going. I was still figuring out where we were. The only thing I knew was we were really close to my father's. The clouds started to come closer to us and I could hear the thunder off in the distance.

I followed Starlin while Grend and Somber followed behind us. Starlin was walking at a quick pace, it seemed as soon I would be right next to her, and her pace quickened even more. She did this over and over again until she was almost at a dead run. "Starlin!" I yelled after her as she ran even faster. I had never seen her run so fast before. "Starlin!" I yelled again angrily, and this time she stopped.

Starlin spun around. "What?" She sounded shocked as to why I was so mad at her. "Why are you yelling at me?" she said, snapping towards me.

"You started to run off. Every time I got close to you your pace quickened until you started at a dead run."

"I was? If I was, why am I not out of breath?"

She was right. We were not that far from the bridge, I was breathing extremely heavily as if I ran miles and miles. Starlin wasn't breathing heavily at all. I turned around and Grend and Somber were right next to us. I had no idea what was going on. Was I still dreaming? I was extremely confused, nothing made sense anymore. My head started to spin, and then everything started to spin.

"Kia." I looked over at Somber as things were spinning and Starlin had her pinned. I saw Grend right next to me kissing my hand. "Why are you doing this?" The last thing I saw before I was out cold on the ground was Grend walking over to Somber and kissing her head.

Chapter Twenty-Six

When I awoke, my head was foggy, everything seemed to be in a cloud. I could tell I was moving, but not by walking, I was in another cage sitting on straw. "Kia?" I looked around, wondering who the male was that said my name. "Kia. It's alright." I could feel a hand touch my face, it was warm and inviting.

"Esom, is that you?" I started to cry.

"Yes, Kia. I'm glad you're safe," he said, wiping a tear from my face.

"Where are we and where are we going? More importantly, how did you get here?"

I looked over towards Esom and saw that he was hurt really badly. He had cuts all over his body and his arms, his wings were in bad shape as well. One wing was missing and the other was torn and mangled. "What happened to you?"

I moved closer to him only to find that I was chained at the waist and couldn't move. I started to wonder what happened to Somber. I looked around for her, only to see that she was right next to me still unconscious. She had her wings wrapped in chains and tied to her waist. Her tail was in chains and tied to her feet, as well as she had a chain around her mouth.

"You still ask a lot of questions," he said, sounding sarcastic as to lighten the mood.

"Well…. You going to answer any of them?"

"First I will tell you that I am deeply sorry for what I did to you. I did not mean to hurt you in anyway. You see I was not myself. As for what happened to me? I was attacked by the Shades. They were wanting information from me as to where you were. I was forced to tell them about you, for that I am sorry. We have been captured by these two imposters," he said as he pointed towards Grend and Starlin.

"What do you mean?"

"This is not Grend and Starlin. Well they are but they are not. Shades took over their bodies in order to get close to us and weaken our guard so they could capture us. As for where we are headed? We are on our way to your father's."

"What?"

"Yes, at least now you don't have to walk." He started to laugh a little.

"Why is that so funny?"

"Sorry, that was rude. We are on our way to your father's," he said, sounding more serious now.

"We need to get out of here and as far away from them as possible."

"How do you suppose we are to do that? We are surrounded by Shades."

I looked around and saw that we indeed were surrounded. All of them in black robes with their piercing one red and one blue eyes. There was only one who was not wearing a robe. As a matter of fact, he looked awfully familiar. The more I stared at him the more I knew I had seen him somewhere before.

He turned and looked at me while slamming his fist on the cage. "Why couldn't you have died in my hands? I wouldn't be here right now, if it wasn't for your mother." I looked at his arm and saw that he had a scar burn where my mother had her hand on him. "You deserve what is coming to you, Princess. Don't worry, your death will be quick."

"How far are we from my father's?" I asked Esom as the Shade turned around and walked away from us.

"I am not sure, maybe a few hours."

"What about Grend and Starlin?"

"I am not sure."

I sat there quietly wondering what was going to happen to us, were we really going to die? I felt as though I had given up going back to my father alive. I didn't want anyone else hurt, I just wanted this all to be over with and get to see my father one last time before he dies and before I do. I am no fighter, I am no savior, I am a princess who has always done what she was told to do by her mother. I might have never listened to my father at all but I don't deserve the throne after what I have put him through.

A female slowly maneuvered around the Shades and drew close to the cage. "My name is Dresia, Princess. I am the right-hand Shade to the Dark Master. Your time to finally help us has come."

I have to get out of this cage. Even though I have given up on my life I can't let Starlin, Somber or the others get hurt any more than they already have because of me, I said to myself.

"I can read your thoughts little princess. You won't be able to keep anything from me or the Dark Master."

"Then do what you must. I can't let you keep hurting innocent people for the purpose of the Dark Master's wish to become the sole ruler of the planet."

"In due time, Princess. The Dark Master still has plans for you."

She moved closer to the moving cage, she seemed to float on the air. She wrapped her tail around my neck and pinned my head to the cage bars. Esom went to get up to help me when Dresia looked towards him, and as his eyes turned to a solid blue he sat back down.

Was Esom working with the Dark Master? I didn't want to think about it for Dresia could read my thoughts. I tried to pull her tail off my neck but the more I tried the tighter she squeezed. When I was on the verge of passing out, Dresia pulled a vial out of her shirt and placed the opening in her mouth to pull off the cap.

She started to laugh as she pulled my mouth open and dumped the vial into it. She laughed even harder as she squeezed my neck tighter. The male who tried to kill me in my dream hurried to Dresia and placed his hand on her shoulder. Dresia's grip loosened slightly.

"You know you can't kill her. The Dark Master has to be the one to do it."

"I know, but it would be so satisfying to kill her for the Dark Master."

"If you did, you know the Dark Master would never forgive you."

"Oh, I would be forgiven. Trust me, I know the Dark Master far more than you do."

"Fine, do as you wish, Dresia."

"Ok…. I'll let her go. You have your wish, Rifarde."

She quickly let me go. I couldn't even muster the strength to cough for air or move my hands to comfort my neck. Everything started to go blurry, I wasn't falling asleep nor was I awake. Whatever Dresia gave me paralyzed me enough so I could see what was going on but I could not move or talk. I could only hear my thoughts which I couldn't control. I started to remember everything from when I was an infant learning how to walk, talk, my first time learning from the scholars, sitting and listening in on my parents yell and fight, meeting Starlin, running away. Everything was flashing and I couldn't control it.

"You see, Kia, I have now gained access to all of your memories. Which will help the Dark Master."

"What do you mean?" I was able to concentrate long enough to think these words to her.

"Oh, don't worry about it, Princess, you will die just like your mother did."

I started to recall images of my mother when she was stabbed in the leg, and watching her die in bed from the sickness of the poison. "So, I will die by poison?"

"Yes, I have already given it to you. It is a stronger dose then the one I used on your mother, but the Dark Master insisted on giving you this much. Don't worry though, I will make sure you stay alive long enough to see your father and the new prince die in front of you as you are then killed by the Dark Master."

The surrounding area became more and more familiar to me. We were getting closer to my home, my father. Everything was hazy, I could not really talk or move. Most of my thoughts were a blur and I could not grasp them. How can the Dark Master make and keep control over so many Shades? My thought echoed in my mind. The girl named Dresia was nowhere to be seen, so I think she was unable to hear my thoughts this time.

When I looked over to Esom he was staring off into the distance as if in a trance. Somber was still asleep, my guess would be from the kiss this fake Grend had given her. I wasn't even sure how long she would be asleep. The sun had fully risen by now and I started to hear the Shades become more excited and moving around a lot more than they were on the way before. We came to an abrupt stop, and I heard yelling in the distance.

Chapter Twenty-Seven

"You are not allowed in here, Shades, go back to wherever it was you crawled from."

"Oh, is that so?" I could hear Dresia speaking to whoever it was who yelled. "Bring her to me."

Rifarde came to the cage, opened it and dragged me from it. I was trying to walk but I couldn't, my legs left like string. I was more or less being dragged by him to where Dresia was.

"Princess! What have you done to her?"

"Never mind that. I will let you in on a secret though. You can either lift this protection spell on the castle walls and let us in so I can heal this little princess of yours, or you can watch her die outside the walls by the poison that is inside her. The choice is yours."

"You're mad. I would never lift the spell for you."

"So be it, you can then watch her die here and explain to her father that you let the heir to the throne die outside the castle walls."

Dresia walked towards me as Rifarde pushed me to the ground. Dresia made an ice and lightning sword from out of thin air, as she walked closer and closer to me. I could feel my heart racing faster and faster the closer she got. She slowly raised her arm holding the sword. "Are you sure you want her to die here?" She looked towards the guard.

"Last chance."

"Never, you will never come in."

"So be it then, she will die."

As she swung her arm down to strike me I heard a male voice yell, "Stop, I'll let the spell down if you let the princess go!"

She stopped right as the blade touched my neck and dug into my skin sending a shock through my body which made me cringe and yell from the pain.

The voice sounded familiar and it took me a minute to remember who he was. It was Fayrel, a spell caster that had been with the royal family for generations. No one knows his true age for he keeps changing when he was born every day.

I could feel myself becoming weaker and weaker, I was having a hard time keeping myself awake. "I will not let her go until you have let us in. Then I will release her to you. You better quickly make up your mind, she only has a little bit longer before she is dead."

"So be it." Fayrel sounded disappointed as he started to mouth a spell that no one could hear.

His hand started to glow and so did the castle, as bright light surround the castle and then quickly disappeared. "Let down the gate. Let them in. Be quick about it." The guards that controlled the gate moved as fast as the wheels would turn and lowered the gate.

"Finally, the Dark Master will control this pathetic planet."

Rifarde put me back into the cart with Somber and Esom, then started to pull us through as Dresia led him and the Shades behind us. Once Dresia, Rifarde and the cart were in the castle the Shades started to follow. Only as soon as they touched the gate entrance they disintegrated on contact. Dresia quickly turned around to see them disappearing. "What is going on?" she said, twitching as each one disappeared. "You think I would be that stupid to let your army in here? I only agreed to let you two in here."

"You will pay for this."

"Now I held up my end, now heal her and let her go."

"A deal is a deal," she conceded with a devilish

smile.

She waved her hand towards me and I started to glow red. I was lifted off the cage floor slightly and then set back down. "There, it's done. Rifarde, let her go."

"You sure?"

"Yes, we are already in the castle." He walked to the cage door and let me out. "What about Somber and Esom?"

"Oh, that is not part of the deal, Princess. I was only to let you go."

"Princess, hurry to the throne room. Your father is waiting for you." Fayrel walked off and disappeared. I was torn between helping Somber and Esom and getting to my father. I started to walk away slowly from them. Dresia was smiling at me mischievously. If I could quickly get to my father before she did this would all be over.

"I'll come back for you. Don't worry."

"Oh. Look at that. She does care. Rifarde, let's head to the king."

Chapter Twenty-Eight

I ran off into the castle hoping that I would beat them to my father. I wasn't sure how they were going to get to the throne room. Even the maids get lost in the maze inside the castle. Unless you have been in the castle your whole life, you would never be able to find it easily. I ran in the entrance and hid behind a tapestry, I pushed on the wall and a door opened up. Once I was through I pushed on a stone in the floor and the door closed behind me.

I needed to quickly get to my father, and this was the most direct route to him. Even inside this passage was still a maze. I only had to make three turns, one right and two left before I stopped at a dead end. I pushed a brick on the wall in front of me and the door opened up. I walked through and I was in the throne room.

I looked up and I saw my father standing next to the throne and the new King standing next to him. "Father," I cried and ran towards him. Before I reached him a cloud of red smoke appeared in front of me. I started to see six figures and knew who it was.

"Where do you think you are going? This throne does not belong to you. It belongs to the Dark Master."

"How did you get in here?"

"Isn't it obvious, we followed you. You see that potion I made you drink, remember it was also a tracking spell."

"I will never let you have the throne."

"We will see about that." With a quick wave of her finger she froze my father and the prince. "Now they won't interfere."

"What have you done to them?"

"Oh, don't worry, Princess, they are just frozen. That way they will not intervene when the Dark Master comes and takes the throne."

I did not know what I was going to do, I had no powers or weapons. "I still will do anything I can to stop you."

"How are you to do that? You are helpless," he said with a giggle.

"With my help." Fayrel walked through the door. "I will make sure that your Dark Master will not take the throne."

"We will see about that one."

Fayrel cast a spell which immobilized Dresia.

"Is that all?" She was not immobilized like he thought, she flicked her tail and sent Fayrel flying backwards hitting the edge of a table. Holding his side which was bleeding badly, he stood.

Electricity formed around his body and shot across the room at Dresia. Starlin jumped in front of Dresia and took the full blast. She fell to the floor coughing up blood. "Good girl, protect me as you all will do." With the flick of her hand, Esom, Somber, Starlin and Grend's eyes glowed red then turned black.

"What have you done to them?" I said throwing a small stone at Dresia as Grend jumped in front of the stone. "I control them, they will do as I say when I say to do it. Rifarde?"

"Yes, Dresia?"

"Let us end this. I'm getting bored here."

"Yes, Dresia."

My friends charged Fayrel, as stones surrounded their feet. Grabbing at the stone as they tried break free. Dresia helped them break free as she just stood and watched them attack Fayrel and I. Fayrel was struggling to maintain control and protect me at the same time. Badly injured with a stab from Rifarde's blade, he fell to the floor.

I stood with what little strength I had, as Esom and Starlin dragged me over to Dresia. "No, you will not harm the princess!" Fayrel mouthed a spell that no one could hear as Dresia started to scream in pain. My friends' eyes were longer black but were glowing red.

"No. You cannot take my toys!" Dresia said as her eyes glowed red as well. She stood as her body was shaking from pain. You could tell she was fighting.

Chapter Twenty-Nine

"Enough... of... this..." A cloud of red smoke started to swirl around Dresia. I watched as her body grew in size from a child to an adult. Her hair was longer and female features more prominent. "Now my powers are fully restored. Fayrel, you will no longer be a problem." I had no idea what she was talking about.

"Sedria?" Fayrel said in shock.

I was wondering who he was talking about.

"It can't be you. Everyone thought you were dead."

"Enough chit chat, this ends now. You might have been my teacher but I can guarantee you that I am much stronger then you will ever be." Her teacher? What was she talking about. He has never left the castle.

Fayrel mouthed the same words again that put Sedria in pain the first time. Sedria laughed. "That will not work this time. My powers have far outgrown yours."

She rushed him as my friends rushed me, with both of us being thrown to the floor. I was being hit left and right with no way to defend myself. Blood started to appear on my clothes and the floor, and I fell to my knees.

Fayrel was doing everything he could to fend off Sedria. With her powers having increased, her magic was crippling him. He fought with everything he had. His magic blows were just like a feather hitting the floor, doing him no good and he knew he was losing. He took one last final breath and screamed at the top of his lungs.

My friends, Rifarde and Sedria glowed white as they were lifted off the ground and thrown in every which way possible. As Fayrel's scream died down they fell to the floor unconscious. Rifarde quickly got up and disappeared.

"Coward," Sedria whispered, as she stood up and

wiped the blood from her face.

"Enough toying." Sedria laughed as she whipped her tail towards him, grabbing him by the neck. He glowed red and blue while shrinking and changing shape. Fayrel's glow moved towards Sedria and formed a pendant around her neck. Sedria continued to laugh and Fayrel stopped glowing.

"What have you done to him?" I said, as I tried to stand on my one good leg.

"Isn't it obvious, he is my personal property now. I am surprised you haven't figured out who I am yet."

"No, I have no idea who you are and I don't want to know."

Chapter Thirty

"Well, sis…"

I cut her off. "Sis?"

"Yes, I am your sister Sedria," she said as she bowed formally.

"I have no sister."

"Oh, but you do, I am also the Dark Master. Here, let me explain it to you. Before you were born our mother and father banished me from the castle and put this barrier up to keep me out. You see, they were scared of me, for what I tried to do to them."

"You lie. They would never have done that. If you are my sister, then why have I never heard of you before or seen any evidence of you in the castle?"

"Will you be quiet." She flicked her hand towards me. I could no longer speak. "There, that's better."

I limped towards the throne.

"I don't think so."

She flicked her tail towards me while waving her hand. Black angel flowers appeared around me out of the cracks in the floor. They started to climb up my legs and eventually covered my whole body. I could feel the thorns dig into me as I tried to move to get out of them. "The more you move the more they will hurt."

"You see, I can take that throne anytime I want to now. You can't stop me. I just want you to know who I am before I kill you. You still are my sister after all. So, let me explain this to you on how I became who I am."

She walked closer to me, and as I looked over at Starlin, Somber, Esom and Grend laying on the floor I started to cry. I didn't know if they were still alive or not. I couldn't see them breathing. Sedria took her hand and placed it on my chin. "You look just like Mother, only you have Dad's eyes."

She let go and walked towards Starlin and with the wave of her hand, Starlin lifted off the ground and moved close to her.

"This here is the real Starlin and that is the real Grend, they have been the whole time. I had my Shades take over their body only to get close to you, and have you bring me home. Since I was never going to be able to enter the castle on my own."

She kissed Starlin and as she pulled her away from her, she inhaled. A black cloud made its way out of Starlin's mouth and started to swirl around her.

"My Shades are me, they are my eyes and my ears. They do my bidding and when I want information from them I absorb them back into myself."

Sedria's eyes went wide.

"This can't be. It was you all along. I could have killed you long ago but I didn't think Mother chose you."

I tried to talk but I couldn't.

"Kia, you were never the heir to the throne. she is," angrily Sedria cried as she turned around towards me. My eyes went wide. How could this be? She is not a princess by blood, only by adoption.

"Kia, we could never have been the heir unless mother chose you. I thought she had chosen you. I found out when I was little that just like Father has to choose an heir to the throne, Mother did too. I asked Mother what would happen to me once the new queen is known and crowned. Mother continued to tell me that we become her servants and her records keeper. Now as you can see that doesn't sound too appealing, does it?"

I started to cry. Mother never told me that before. I couldn't believe what I was hearing.

"Oh, what I am saying is true, remember I can still

hear your thoughts only when I want to. She probably didn't tell you because of what happened when she told me. I didn't want to become a servant to anyone. I wanted to become queen. I remembered the story Mother told me about if the heir didn't sit on the throne and become queen anyone can, so we had to protect the new heir. She told me that I was not to know how the new heir was chosen only that once she is, she will be protected by the family. So, I devised a plan to kill Mother and Father and become the first sole ruler of the planet before they chose the new heirs and they sat upon the throne."

She threw Starlin up against the wall and impaled her in the shoulder. I tried to move towards her. "I was really close to killing Mother when Father caught me in the act. They were both furious with me, that is when they banished me from the castle. In order to keep me from killing them, Fayrel put a barrier up to keep me and anything that works for me out. But that didn't last that long. I knew Mother would eventually come out of the castle. That is when I approached her in Tebar, and I tried to reason with her. When that didn't work, I stabbed her with a blade made out of the same poison that is inside of you. The only reason why his barrier works is because Fayrel is the first king who ruled this planet."

How is that possible? I wondered hoping she would hear me.

"Ah, good question. You see, just like the first Queen putting a spell on the royal family, Queens and Kings to become fairies and protect the knowledge of the planet. She had another job for her King. She made him immortal so he could protect the royal family. As you can see."

She tapped the pendant around her neck. "That didn't work out too well for him. He has become weak in his old, old age."

She started to laugh.

"I knew the only way that I was going to be able to get into the castle was to get to you and use you to enter. Once Fayrel saw that you were about to die he would let me in. After all, he was ordered to protect you."

Chapter Thirty-One

A sword appeared in Sedria's hand, and as it was thrown towards me, I flinched and closed my eyes thinking this was the end. I could feel the tip of the sword touch me. When I opened my eyes, Somber was between me and the sword. "No! How did you awaken?"

Somber fell to the floor with the tip slicing the vines. I fell along with her catching her head before it landed on the ground.

"Oh well, one less person to kill later." She flicked her hand and the sword pulled out of Somber and returned to Sedria. "Kia, is that you? I can't see."

"Yes, it's me."

"Good, you're safe."

"Why did you do that?"

"You saved my life, now it was my turn to save yours. I heard everything she said. I couldn't move to help you though. Once I saw what she was about to do, I used the last bit of strength I had to protect you. Here."

She grabbed her tail and ripped it off, transforming her tail into a flaming sword. "You must kill her."

I took the sword from her, she closed her eyes and stopped breathing. I looked up at Sedria and I saw Esom behind her slowly standing up. I knew what I had to do, kill my so-called sister and end this war. I started to charge towards her with the sword. Sedria laughed. "You think you can kill me?"

Just then Esom rushed her and wrapped his arms around her pinning her. "What are you doing? This won't work. You can't hurt me."

"Want to bet?" Esom said coughing blood. He took

his sword and ran it though her. As she gasped, she looked down to grab the sword. I ran quicker towards her and ran the sword through her heart. She looked at me and just smiled.

She started to glow red, and so did Somber. "This isn't over." With an exhale, she closed her eyes and vanished with Somber.

I heard a faint echo of Fayrel's voice. "Princess, sorry I couldn't protect you."

I knelt down next to Esom. "You're going to be ok."

He just smiled at me and closed his eyes.

A figure appeared in front of me, it looked like a ghost of Fayrel. He walked over to the prince and my father, and with a slight touch they started to move. He walked over to Grend and Esom, bending down to touch them. When they awoke they no longer had any scratches or blood on them. He flicked his hand at Starlin and lowered her down from the wall, healing her wound before she touched the floor.

He turned to me and touched my forehead. "Sorry this is all I could do."

I felt a warm sensation rush over me as Fayrel vanished. I raced over to Starlin as she opened her eyes. "Kia... How did we get here? Last thing I remember was being in the fairy kingdom."

"We are home."

"How did that happen?"

"Long story, but now is not the time for that. You need to go take your place as Queen Starlin."

"What, me? No, you are the Queen."

"No, she is not, Starlin, you are. Kia cannot become the queen for she is not a full-blooded Skin. You are, and only a full-blooded Skin and a full-blooded Scale can become a Queen or King. That is the way of the treaty," my father said calmly to her.

She didn't know what to say, Starlin slowly walked towards the throne. "It is tradition for the Scale to sit first," Father said. The Prince sat on his throne as he glowed white. When the white subsided and there was a crown on top of his head, "Hail the King," Father announced.

Starlin walked up to her throne, when she was inches from touching it she stopped as she stumbled a few steps. Her head rolled off her shoulders and fell as Rifarde slowly walked out from behind the throne standing tall and proud.

I went to rush to Starlin when my skin started to crawl, it became tighter as I clawed at my body. I slowly sat down on the floor as my skin turned gray. A black angel flower appeared in front of me, while its vine traveled up my legs. A thorn pierced my skin as a single drop of blood fell into the center of the flower as my skin got darker. My veins throbbed as I struggled to breathe. Everything slowly turned black as the vines completely surrounded me. I felt my body convulse as I started to wither with the vines. My body crumbled into dust as Rifarde picks up the black angel flower and vanished.

Don't forget to check out the next in the Series coming soon.

Skin and Scale

White Angel Flower

Chapter One

Watching as a pair of hummingbirds fly past my window twisting and turning around each other as though dancing, heading through the trees of the Foy Forest.

In the center of the forest resides the sacred field of white angel flowers. In the distance, a single budding flower starts to glow a soft white as the pedals slowly open reviling a small red and purple speckled egg.

The hummingbirds fly towards the egg. As one hovers over, the other one lands. Tilting its head as it examines the egg. With each movement it flaps its wings as if removing any bugs that may be on the egg.

Suddenly a shadow starts to slowly creep over the egg. In a blink of an eye it quickly vanishes, as all you could hear is a little girl's laughter slowly echoing off into the distance. The two hummingbirds start to franticly fly around the egg as the petals close. A light snow starts to fall covering only the ground around the flower. The hummingbirds flying in a pattern over the now closed flower start to glow along with the flower. One glowing purple while the other one red.

Slowly circling down towards the flower, there movements gain speed as the flower again glows a soft white. After landing on the flower, the soft white glowing subsides. The flower now starts to pulse a soft red, purple, and white color. Like a heartbeat the colors rotate.

With a small flap of the wings the hummingbirds stop moving. Their color starts to fade turning them grey as stone. Attached to the flower they have become stone statues. As if guarding the precious egg and what lays inside.

######

"My mother was so stupid."

"Why do you say that?"

"Well she gave me everything that I needed."

I walk to the center of the room while picking up the black angel flower that was laying on the table. Staring into the bubbling white cauldron hanging over the fire. "My sister here is only part of the key." Looking over towards the lifeless Somber on the floor.

"She is the final key. I still need more ingredients to make this work."

"I will get you anything you need Sedria."

Walking around the cauldron, I reach my hands out towards his face. Pulling him towards me, we kissed as I dropped the flower from my hand. He quickly catches the flower and pulls away from me.

"You might not want to destroy this, dropping it might not seem like a bad idea. Just remember even the smallest crease in the petal can alter the spell."
Handing me the flower.

"Your right, how clumsy of me. You know I couldn't have killed Starlin or my sister without you. My love."

"Your love?" Shocked, he stares at me blankly.

"Yes, I have always had feelings for you. When you didn't know who I was, and I played the part as Dresia. I thought of you all the time. I didn't want to tell you who I was though. I didn't want you to think of me differently."

"I would do anything for you. It does not make a difference to me if you were Dresia or Sedria, even though you truly are both." Leaning towards me he kisses me slightly on the forehead.

My head starts to spin, as I grasp at my chest. Breathing heavy I stumble back words and sit on the chair that I am grasping at to keep my balance.

"Sedria, you need to rest. I know that you cannot be killed but you still feel a great deal of pain. Please, rest."

"You're right, I will. Can you help me to my room?"

With an ever so gentle hand, he helps me up as he lets me put all my weight on him. We walk towards my room; the hallway is laced with candles no furniture or windows can be seen only laced curtains and few decorations.

Once outside my door, I let go and reach for the doorknob tripping over my feet. He catches me and opens my door while the helps me over to my bed. After laying me down, he kisses me ever so slightly then turns to walk out of the room as I close my eyes falling asleep.

To be continued…

www.ingramcontent.com/pod-product-compliance
Lightning Source LLC
Chambersburg PA
CBHW071926220626
47052CB00002B/470